CW01593964

# Frontier Writers
# The Gold of the Day

edited by Frontier Writers



Published by Frontier Writers
Cumbernauld, UK
ISBN: 978-1-906306-11-3

First printing, November 2009

Font: Tahoma 12 pt

Cover design: Frontier Writers

www.frontierwriters.com

# The Gold of the Day

## A Collection of Poetry and Prose

δ

# Contents

δ

δ

## Introduction

Since the publication of their first anthology in 2007, Frontier Writers have gone from strength to strength. Their work has made it into print in mainstream publications, short story showcase pamphlets, online anthologies and internet niches. Some members have experimented with performance poetry, bringing the group's work to a new audience.

Since its rebirth in 2006, the writers have supported each other in their endeavours, by listening, editing and giving feedback; always in a useful and constructive manner. The group supports writers who have just begun their journey as scribblers, those who are old hands, having immersed themselves in poetry and prose for decades and those who are at various destinations along the route; still travelling, albeit at differing velocities. The group's inclusive and open nature encourages members to feel at home and part of the team whether they are still at the bus stop, or waiting for the rest to catch up.

This anthology represents work from all of those members. Some of the pieces turned up in need of a good scrub and polish, some were burnished like gold, and so blindingly shiny that the editing committee needed sunglasses. Some had to be coaxed in the door like their owners. They all represent what Frontier Writers is about. The group is diverse. It is welcoming. But above all it strives to make every member a better writer.

We hope you the reader enjoy our work presented in this collection, *The Gold of the Day*.

*Frontier Writers, November 2009*

# Hatched

Danny O'Connor

I remember the very day I was hatched. My memories started with the feeling of a warm darkness and an incessant whistling inside my brain like the mating call of a randy cock-linnet.

My head started rocking back and forth in time with the tune and the rhinocap on my forehead tap, tapped against the inside of my shell. My shoulders were hunched and I was cramped inside my embryo growing-space. By a combination of the rhythmic tapping of my forehead and the stretching of my limbs, I cracked my shell from the inside.

As the vacuum broke, I gulped in my first lungfulls of air. The shell crumbled around my head and I felt the breeze hit my cheek. The ions in the air attacked the protective crystalline crust around my eyes, and with me blinking furiously, the swimming world soon focussed into reality.

But my first sight was not my doting dad, like it says in all the Best Baby Books, but, there was I, ready to imprint on a red leatherette barstool, standard public house issue since the year dot. I repeat, the first thing I saw through the batwing doors of the Last Chance Saloon was this bloody barstool. If the 'vision' had've lasted too much longer, until my skin had dried, according to the Baby Book, then I would have fixated on the barstool as my daddy and no amount of aversion therapy would've induced me from taking up my 'rightful' place behind the bloody stool, ready to follow it, with unquestioning loyalty, wherever it chose to lead me.

I only have to close my eyes and I can see the whole scene in front of me. Standing proud and shiny, eighteen inches off the floor, was this brass foot-rail and sitting on the washed out Formica bar top was Daddy's half-gulped pint of heavy with a wee goldie by its side. My absent father's fag was smoking away in its ash tray within his, not seen, arms reach. Dad had popped to the loo to relieve his three-pint bladder, but had got talking to one of his buddies in the khazie and just plumb forgot the time.

So there I was mewling and crying in this old pram with bits of broken shell all around me and the thing which was getting imprinted in my brain was this old red barstool, with daddy nowhere in sight. The pram was a hand-me-down. I think my great aunt Matilda was the original occupant and mine was about the fifteenth bum to be sitting in it. It had the old penny-farthing style wheels and the boat-shaped basin and back-facing rain-hood. You know the type. All those photo-realist documentaries have scarf-headed women pushing dirty washing in them. This pram was so old it didn't even have the mandatory cargo-net to hold the egg in place if the brakes failed and it went careering down a hill.

Anyway, this nightmare scenario of being imprinted on to an inanimate object stopped as soon as dad's baldy head zoomed into my vision. While his left hand tickled me under the chin, his right deftly twisted the rhino-cap off my forehead without even leaving a scar.

Every time I think of my old man I get this vision of that bloody barstool and a half-finished pint of heavy and I can taste, again, the stale cigarette smoke that chokes the back of my throat.

# John Went to Tahiti

William N. Dyer

He called the funeral director, the estate and travel agents on the same day.
His mother went out in style.
She would have been content with her son's offering, happy for his escape.

He sold the fish 'n' chip shop, and booked a passage to Tahiti;
Polynesian voices not strange but inviting.
If someone was to blame it was Paul Gauguin.

He took a pen and lots of paper - there was no sadness in his life.
He had done his duty and was satisfied
The dream would come to pass.

He wrote his novel with nobody's help.

# Milk of Human Kindness

Jacqueline Woods

She's got some milk! She's putting it on the ground...she's still standing there...should I come out from under the bush? She *looks* friendly...one paw...two paws...one two three four! Aaaaaaaaaaaaah. Cool and creamy! Mmmmmmmmm. She's still standing there. She's bending down. She's making some funny, sooky, baby noises. Humans are so silly! I'm a full grown cat. But I suppose it *does* mean she likes me. I'll try some purring. That usually works a treat. Hhrhrhrhrhrhrrrrrrr. A hand is presented. A quick sniff. Mmmmm. Smells clean and sweet. And of food. I'll let it touch me.

The back of the hand, held motionless, a hair's length away. My nose twitches. My hairs bristle on my head. Oh, so close, so thrilling. A sweet rippling shiver of hair, standing up in greeting. But I wait, I savour. I draw the hand towards my head. It will come to me. It cannot resist. It touches! First the outer, standing hairs, then the hand and head move together, almost from my nose and then back, down to my shoulders. So bold and daring for a first stroke. Does the Hand think I'm anyone's? Oh, so warm and soft and kind. At this very moment, nothing exists except the Hand and I.

The females are the best to court, and much more often fall for my feline wiles. I think I'll let it touch me again.

So sweet and gentle and caring a touch. Hhrhrhrhrhrrrrrrrrrrrr... I know most definitely I am a human cat, not a feral feline, with muddy paws. And she is a cat's human. She belongs to me. I will amuse her, give her comfort, and take her or leave her as I please. I will cultivate her affection; it may be very useful to me. The hand will eventually present me with food, if I perform affection and playfulness well.

An open palm now moves gently but firmly from my forehead, over my ears, squashing them down playfully on the way, down my neck, along my back, and keeps going, as it pulls gently along my out-stretched tail, to the very tip. We both enjoy the luxury of the contact, the Hand and I. But in a second or two, I will disengage myself, and leave it wanting more, and trot away with purpose. I have a busy life, and I will let the Hand know it. Places to go, humans to enthral.

Just as I am about to trot away, when the senses of touch and smell are so full and gorged, and I feel so soft and sweet and that this hand is quite useful, and I will definitely come back to it, and I would quite like to lick it, and taste it, and find out just how sweet it is...it disappears. The human has towered up again and has stopped making all the silly noises, and the other strange noises that mean, I think, that it is trying to communicate, though why would *I* want to understand its foolish language and thoughts? It goes inside.

With a twitch of ear and whisker, and quick lick of paw, *my* paw tastes sweeter; I do not need to lick a human, I turn in the direction of the hole in the fence. I am free to roam, and freedom gives me choice. I will choose another garden. But I have not taken one step, when the human comes outside again, and there is the smell of..................fish!

There is no mistaking the declaration of fish in the air. Perhaps I will stay a little longer. This seems quite a promising human. Fish from a human dish is quite a feast, compared to the milk and scraps in other gardens. But I will still play the gardens, play the humans, play the game. I wouldn't want to disappoint any of them. I'll give them just enough affection to bring a little smile to their dreary lives. I'll let them give me food if I want it, and a stroke if I feel in the mood. I suppose I can't let them down, if they're expecting me, and keep looking for hours and hours forlornly and pathetically through the transparent wall in the house, in to the garden, from the inside to the world outside, for a sign of their feline friend. It is nice to be wanted. It is nice to wind them round my curly tail. Which one shall I choose? Or which ones? As I casually lick my lips and follow this human inside, I wonder which house has the cosiest corners, and the richest, most plentiful food. Only one way to find out: I will let her, and each one, display and provide samples of their assets. And only then will I decide, if any at all, which will be my human.

Of course, I can never become too attached. That would never do. I am my own cat, just as it should be. But for now, and as a matter of feline nature, I will survey my various kingdoms, and let my human subjects pay me homage...and partake of some more delicious fish!

# One of Us

Claire Szemis

*September, 1954*

I do not often turn down a cigar.

It is one of those out of the ordinary treats that I allow myself now and again, when I am either feeling quite downtrodden and urgently require something more than the standard tobacco, or when it is a very important occasion; Christmas, for example. I always enjoy a cigar after an outstanding festive feast, when the turkey and black pudding are uncomfortably pressing in my stomach. *He* and I would sit in our respective and preferred armchairs and light each other's with a sated, exhausted sigh, and I would pour my favourite festive tipple.

So I would not often knock back a rather generous offer of hand-wrapped Cubans in exchange for an evening of office politics. Bradbury had invited me, you see. He is getting extraordinarily anxious in his old age, as I have noted before in previous journal entries. Bradbury has not been quite the same individual since someone claimed he was not "one of us," and though he denied any involvement, declaring he could not speak a word of

Russian, there would seem to be a lot of the facts against him. But he has not been passing information to the Kremlin; no it is spectacularly more serious than that. He has been consorting with the French.

No matter what he's done it will probably just end up swept under the carpet like a lot of other things around here. There has been too much scandal of late; it will be hushed up, smothered, and in a year Bradbury will be forced into early retirement. I do not feel particularly sorry for him if he has been messing around with them across the Channel. I think he sees me as some sort of ally though, I cannot for the life of me begin to imagine why, and around lunchtime he was hanging around my office like a bad smell, promising me those fine cigars and a rather expensive brand of scotch that I am partial to but can never afford myself.

Maybe he felt sorry for me, which is even more reason to decline such offers in the future. I do not want, nor am I looking for any sympathy. It is not as if my sister has died, she's just... gone. Sometimes I come home from work and there will be something missing from the house; her umbrella for example, that red coat that she loved to wear in Autumn and I'll know she's come back to collect more of her things and gone away again. I am just thankful she has not ran off with HIM, as *he* has quite definitely disappeared, and *he* will stay gone if he knows what is good for him.

I have my suspicions that she is staying with Lydia; that woman is just as empty headed and silly as Mary and no doubt they are having a grand time discussing me contemptuously. Mary will come back eventually when she has run out of money, she always comes back then, but of course I keep a good tight grip on mine. Money runs through her fingers like water. It annoys her exceedingly that I somehow always have a little to spare. She said I was always so Scottish with my money, and I had to correct her with the appropriate alternative adjective. I am sensible, she is not.

The house seems terribly lonely without her though. And without *him*. My parents have asked a few times why we fell out but I cannot go into it right now. I'm still trying to make sense of it in my own head, never mind trying to explain it to others, especially not my father, the Detective Inspector. He was always able to tell more so than my mother when I was lying, or concealing something, but then he deals with liars every day of his life. He has years of experience, and I decided it was better to say nothing at all than deal with him right now.

I do not know why I am finding it so damn difficult at the moment. *He* was my best friend of course but what happened should not have depressed me this much. Apparently it's showing in my face, in my clothes and even in the way I am standing. I overheard as much yesterday when my secretary was coming back from lunch with the other girls, speaking in that strange maternal voice she uses for those in difficulty.

"He is not himself at all," was what she said, and I groaned to myself when the others sighed so sadly on my behalf, "his shirt is all crumpled, those trousers are not pressed right. He is not taking care of himself. And it breaks my heart to see him so forlorn. You know I almost hugged him this morning when he appeared. He is just so... sad."

The last thing I need is my secretary clinging to me. She is a lovely woman and rather pretty in her way. *He* always flirted with her whenever he visited my office. But then *he* flirted with anything in a skirt and my secretary has a thing about those seamed stockings. You know, that line that runs right up the back of the calf and thigh? Those were *his* particular favourite. Mary started wearing them more often; now I know why.

In an effort to convince them otherwise that I am fine, I volunteered to be the umpire tomorrow afternoon for another round of the departmental championship. It'll be the Home Office against the Foreign, and of course I will tend to favour my own boys. There will probably be a lot of angry memos from the Foreign Office on my desk on Monday morning but by then I will most likely be nursing a hangover and be unable to care. Appleby has invited me for dinner with his wife on Sunday, and that man is capable of drinking more than you think he could, and he does it without you realising he has. You think he has only one or two but somehow half the bottle is gone and he will be slightly slurring the end of words. I do not like his wife very much, and it will feel rather odd, just the three of us, but I appreciate the gesture nonetheless.

It's nice to discover that you still have friends.

I sometimes wonder why I even considered *him* my friend, but then it has only been fifteen days since it happened so naturally I am still sore about it. Just thinking about *him*, picturing *his* face gives me indigestion. I'd have done anything for *him*, but now? It would not have hurt half this much if *he* had died. It's the betrayal that gets me most and I got so angry this morning thinking about *him* that I forgot my briefcase and only realised I had done so when I stepped into my office. I want to put *him* out of my mind but I cannot. I cannot forget, not ever.

We were like brothers, but obviously our friendship meant more to me than it did to *him*. Otherwise *he* would never have done what he did. All the gifts *he* ever gave me feel like empty gestures; from the brass magnifying glass and its matching brass letter opener that sit snug in the suede lining of the wooden display box on my desk, to this very diary. I am quite thankful I am reaching the end of the book so I can buy another and start afresh. It pains me every time I open up this one and catch glimpses of happier times within the pages; the more innocent, naive John Hawthorne laughing at me. The front page still bears *his* scrawl; "From J.V. to J.H."

*He* was never "one of us." I tried my best to integrate *him*; from clothing to employment to intellectual improvement. But *he* was one of those jigsaw pieces that never quite fit in with the rest of the picture, as if it was put into the box by mistake. My father quite liked *him* for that reason. The Detective Inspector never understood the desire to fit in with the rest of the crowd. As far as he was concerned, everyone else stole, lied, and murdered so why would anyone want to be like everyone else? My father fights against the rest of the world and my friend did not belong with the rest of the world; they got on extremely well. I wonder what the Detective Inspector would say if I told him just how different HE was.

I suppose I should be thankful that I am rid of *his* bad influence. It was a swift and violent parting, like the amputation of a gangrenous limb. Painful and over so quickly that neither of us had much time to think about it. I did come off worse; that left eye is still quite tender, but *he* is the one on the run, not me, and as such I have been able to sit and think about everything and how we went from one state of affairs to something completely different. There are a few things I still do not understand, but I do not have enough data to theorise with and I must wait until

Mary shows herself in order for me to build a clearer picture. I remember quoting to *him* once, "Data! Data! Data! I can't make bricks without clay!" but that only made him laugh.

Even if I figure out every little detail, what am I supposed to do anyway? I cannot approach anyone with my story; no one would believe it. They say that truth is stranger than fiction but in this case the truth is not strange, it is ridiculous. I would become a laughing stock if I told anyone what I know. But if I do not, there will be no justice, and *he* will have gotten away with it entirely. Perhaps it's my father in me but it will stick in my throat if *he* goes Scot-free.

Something has to be done about *him*; *he* has to be stopped before it can happen to anyone else. Sometimes I fear that I have made a grave mistake, that I did not see what I thought I did, and that I lost my best friend over nothing. But the problem preys on my nightmares, staring at me with accusing eyes, asking when I will solve this terrible problem, and I know I did see it. I did discover *his* secret, as terrible as it is, and the only one who can do anything about it is the one who stares out of the mirror at me every morning.

I do not even know where to begin, and now that I am almost alone in the world, barring those good enough to remain my friends, I suppose this will be a mission I undertake myself. It will require a lot of research and a lot of detective work although my experience in that area is limited. My own abilities, such as they are, are garnered from my childhood years listening to my father and from my ceaseless enjoyment of crime novels.

I did discover something this evening however. My mother used to say that every day was a school day and it seems she may have been right in that sentiment. I know what my own and even Mary's look like because the Detective Inspector once dipped our fingers in ink and smudged our fingertips on pieces of paper. The whisky glass HE favoured and the cigarette case HE left behind possess an entirely different set, and I must confess that I smiled to see it.

Even vampires leave fingerprints.

# You

## Catherine Baird

Every poem is addressed to You.
You, the one I love, the one I hate
The one I would murder given the chance
The one I dream about when I am sleeping.
I love you, I wait for you.
And 'You', sitting there in your pink candlewick dressing gown,
who exactly are 'You'?
Is the poetic 'You' just the one person?
Some poor soul who gets it in the neck from every poet with a grievance?
And is 'You' some sick, fed-up somebody
who has to endure messages of love, love, undying bloody love,
and 'how you set my heart racing' and 'I love the feel of your skin'
and 'what I would do to you if only 'You' were here'
and 'oh god oh god I looooove 'You'.
If that 'You' is the one person then oughtn't we to give 'You' a break?
Poor 'You'.

## Verbal Fisticuffs

James A. Stewart

Ah'll boot yer baws
Naw, ah'll pull yer hair

Whit de ye mean, ya sissy?
Pulling hair? Ya pure wummin

Ah'll get ma uncle, he's in the polis
He can batter anybody
So whit dae ye say,
bawbag?

Ma uncle's in the polis tae
'n he runs the boxing club
Chuck Norris is feart
o' him

Aye, right
Talk shite
Ma da wid batter your da
End o' story

Bring it oan
'cos ma da's a ninja

# Erin the Brave

J. B. Quinn

Languishing
Supinely silver upon the sofa
Slanketly
Vegetating greenly with gusto
Creeping
Silently along the pale, beige carpet
Scuttling
With dark intent towards me
Horror
As shock-blue recognition dawns
Paralysis
Within scarlet, terror-filled eyes
Primal
Scream from black, deep within
Halts
Monstrous-brown, arachnid bastard
Cavalry
Attack with pink Wellington boots
Rescued
Swiftly, by golden Erin the Brave

# Vehicle of Containment

Catherine Baird

For Adam McCabe

Proud, swell, you cannot tell who it will be.
Now holding on in readiness to hold
Indications of temperament in kicks
and future career as football legend
A recipe, cooked up in parent's arms
tender love, and hope, the main ingredients
and fear, and worry, mixed with trepidation
with a dash of sweet anticipation.
You were loved before you even were.
Before your mother knew that you were sure.
before your father heard your beating heart,
when only nature knew who you would be.
And now you're here it all makes perfect sense;
You, holding our future in your wee hands.

# Betrayal

J. B. Quinn

From a natural landscape
'Red in tooth and claw'
The ancient, girl-child arose
Illuminating the spark of enlightenment
Igniting the primitive place
With endless possibilities
Beginning the transformation
Under the old, sincere oak
The ancient, girl-child slept
Captivated by constant summers
Heightened by hormonal pleasures
And the romantic rush of endorphins
Under the spell of a midnight sky
Seduced by treacherous love
The ancient, girl-child wept
Her brave, bright mind descended
Into the darkest realm of reality
Making nightmares of her wildest dreams
Ancient feminine, no more a girl
The daisy chain that grew
Beneath your once, nimble fingers
Has become a noose for your neck

And shackles, to confine your imagination
To the endless repetition of mindless drudgery
Mother of creative consciousness
You lifted the fallen on to their feet
Your strong and gentle touch
Soothed the uncivilised, savage beast
Your pearl-cream milk of kindness
Gave sustenance to the fruit of your womb
Now, awaken to your betrayal
You gave birth to your own death.

# Savages

James A. Stewart

I had an insipid throb in my head, the one that makes its appearance just before the full onset of the inevitable hangover. My senses were dulled by the thought of the impending nausea and the regurgitations that would have to be crossed before I could turn the corner toward the promised land of sensory equilibrium. I could picture the yellow-green bile in my head and the vision served only to hasten the reflux.

"Never again", I mumbled as I walked, nay stumbled, naked toward to the toilet. The reassuring cold of the porcelain made for an unlikely ally in the battle that raged inside me. It, and the tiles, cooled my sweats and gave me hope that I would recover; that this was just a drunkard's phase, and that by evening I'd be ready to do it all again. The reality check came in the form of half digested curry and some nameless foodstuffs that I have no recollection of having eaten anyway. Perhaps more pertinently, I had no desire to recall how they came to be in my stomach which by this stage was spinning like the waltzers that had once adorned the garishly lighted funfairs of the last century.

The curry couldn't have caused this, could it? It was made with the best cuts of meat; only the breast and thigh had been used, De la Croix had assured me of this. It was he who encouraged me, saying that the rewards far outweighed the risks. "You'll feel amazing," he told me with great certainty. His Gallic countenance had persuaded me to try again. So I did. De la Croix didn't so much request as order, even if he did make you think that it was your choice; all part of his vicious charm.

The last time had been just over a year ago and the memory of the cold sweats from then rushed back like a runaway train. Despite The Cook's obvious talent, the bottom-line was that meat in this part of the world had a distinctive toughness to it and no manner of spice or herb could cure this coarseness.

You must understand for someone of my ilk, this was a salvation that I had to attempt. The trigger-happy goons of the Greater War had created a nuclear fallout from their indiscriminate bombings that had left Europe pockmarked and lifeless. The residue of the bombings had wasted no time in traversing the Atlantic before covering the East coast with an angry cloud of radiation, the impact of which resulted in the New Order decreeing a no-one out policy with only one exception: pregnant women. The world to the West was being rebuilt, the rumours had spread to us that there were new buildings, government, law and order and family life. On the East coast things were different, things were how we were told they were to be. It was a lawless and hellish world. I longed for a life in the West and the only way out was to get pregnant and get to a New Order command post and prove I was with child.

The slight complication that greeted this want and opportunity for personal emancipation was that the radiation cloud created by the leaders of this once great nation had left almost all who slumber under her infertile, and for all I knew, that included me.

What I did know was that De la Croix was already getting bored with me. He controlled this irradiated, corner of New Jersey. It was his. We were his. He already had a new plaything in tow and I could see him fawning over her the way he did with me in the early days. Back in my pomp I was gorgeous and whilst I was still pretty, I was ageing and more importantly the alarm on my biological clock was not far from sounding. The differences between how she looked and how she came into his court and favour, versus my arrival, were as stark as they were worrying. I remember only too well the fate that befell my predecessor and it seemed I was heading toward the perishable goods category in double-quick time.

De la Croix was an opportunist and by luck had arrived here just prior to the onset of the conflict that had left half the planet lifeless and uninhabitable. He had escaped death by fleeing Europe and had found his fiefdom waiting. He was as unstable as he was merciless. Nothing stood in his way as he set about taking control of most of the land between Atlantic City and Cape May. As if to prove his implacability to any who would dare challenge his authority he would order the severed heads of his enemies' children to be taken on a continual tour of his territory. This chilling demonstration of his rancour served to make potential antagonists think long and hard before taking action. His ruthlessness earned him the justified respect of all in the region. He wanted for nothing, almost.

He craved a child more than anything – his European heritage gave him the desire to create a monarchical legacy here. Despite his French name and lineage, he claimed a direct link to the Habsburgs who had once ruled vast tracts of Southern and Eastern Europe, and he pledged to rebuild their empire, starting in New Jersey. Me? I wanted a child to escape. We had the same needs but wished for different outcomes – and with medical knowledge scarce on the ground it was impossible to do fertility tests. This left De la Croix looking for alternative means to increase his chances of fathering an heir. The alternative came in the form of The Cook, a Jamaican witch doctor who had grown from lowly chef to De la Croix's right hand man.

The curry was meant to work for us, The Cook was sure of it. I couldn't even recall having sex last night and that was not a good omen. I do recall drinking as much brew as I could before going down for dinner, though. It was clear The Cook's curry was a piece of black magic borne of no real substance. There was no way dining on this concoction was going to magic my ovaries into life. In addition, if De la Croix hadn't killed the last competent doctor in this region, then he may have been able to sire an heir. The doctor had been murdered for daring to suggest De la Croix's chances of fathering a child were slim. It was after this act that he started listening to The Cook's stories of the magic of the Caribbean. I had offended The Cook last year by japing his wonder stories of automatic pregnancy based on food, and most likely I was at it again at the sitting last night. With no De la Croix in my room this morning it was a sensible assumption that I had come home alone.

Despite my place in his court, it was a sham existence. I never wanted to be here, I just was. I never wanted him, circumstance pushed me into his arms, a trade between territorial rivals had priced me at one-hundred acres. A red button pressed in a bomb shelter in some mountain complex out West had put invisible walls around my life and restricted me to one where my body and mind existed in entirely different worlds. I was free to think what I wanted. But in the end, I was only free to do what De la Croix demanded.

I had ruminated all day as to what the mistakes of last night may have been. Then, a knock, his knock, one long tap and two short taps, came gently at my door. I glanced out of the bay window in my room which overlooked the Atlantic Ocean. The sea's brilliant blue hue belied the fact that its vast expanse carried no fish, no plankton, no cetaceans or any other animal activity for that matter. The waves crashing ashore were lifeless, yet still awe-inspiring. The serenity of the view was destroyed by the grim reality of the situation. For a second time a knock came at my door, the same rhythm as before only more insistent. I could feel the affection beyond the door but it was outweighed by the distance in the taps, those three gentle taps on oak. I opened the door and standing there, silhouetted against the candles burning in the hallway, were three figures. It was De la Croix, his New Toy and The Cook complete with a malevolent toothy smile that reflected off of his knives. I knew I'd be at dinner again tonight, but would not be dining.

# Pollice Verso

Alexander J. Cunningham

Cindy looks up from the magazine, surveying her environment with the eyes of a predator. The café is a few blocks from her next venue and she has fifteen minutes or so to spare. In spite of what she's about to do, she is very calm. Even as she lifts her coffee, there are no signs of tremor in her small but powerful hands.

"Yes, there's a fight circuit in the city," Cindy says, confirming what I already suspect. "There's a fight circuit in every city. Finding it, though? That's the hard part. Money will cover any other eventualities," she adds with another smile.

The kind of smile you put in a glass by the side of the bed, before sleeping. That and reconstructive surgery have repaired a lot of the damage she's sustained over the years. But the scars will never truly leave her. Her face, her entire body, bear the ghosts of every punch, slap, bite, kick, stamp, scratch, slash, stab, burn and more: testaments to punishment and pain.

"It's warm in here," Cindy says, shrugging off her coat and escaping its damp folds of cloth. She's wearing blue jeans and a cropped t-shirt, exposing arms and an abdomen bereft of even the slightest ounce of body fat.

The thin, thin skin stretched taut over bundles of twitching muscles.

Fighting weight.

She glances past her reflection in the large windows and out into the rain-swept night. "I hope the weather doesn't keep away the big spenders."

A waitress approaches, delivering a slice of cherry pie to an older man sitting in the next booth, before reaching Cindy. "What can I get you, hon?"

Cindy glances at the menu, then looks up at the older woman standing waiting, order pad in hand, pen poised. "Anything with lots of chocolate in it."

The waitress smiles, a touch of envy in her eyes, knowing such blatant disregard for calories is the reserve of the young or the extremely fit. She scribbles something in her pad and walks away.

"I've been working for three years and I'm good at what I do," Cindy says, looking around the café again. She tells me this without pride or satisfaction. It's merely a statement of fact. "But I'm not the best. Someday, someone will get the better of me. At one end, they'll offer cheaper rates for a session, at the other, they'll simply be better. Faster, tighter and more able than I am."

Cindy picks up the sugar dispenser and upends it over her coffee, letting several spoons worth pour into the thick black liquid.

"And I accept that. It's part of my trade and part of the world I live in." She pauses, think for a moment, then quotes: "'One step sideways of classic Darwinian thinking, but running parallel, with only a fine line between us separating man and beast.'"

Cindy smiles her hard, plastic smile, then adds, "Anthros not included."

*Flesh will pound flesh.*

*Cindy's fists will hammer into the ruined features of the ex-policewoman. Over and over, each punishing blow will elicit a greater and greater response from the rabid, screaming onlookers. And when the ex-policewoman finally goes limp, slumping out of Cindy's grip, the crowd will roar with one voice. A frenzied din that will echo through the derelict factory. Cindy will raise her bloodied fists, basking in their praise, knowing all too well the fickle nature of their adoration.*

*Then a hush will descend like a pall.*

*Breathless, the spectators will wait, wanting, wishing for the final act. The real reason they're there.*

*Wiping blood, both hers and her opponent's, from her own face, Cindy will look around the wide circle of sweating, eager faces. Politicians will be jostling with criminals, whores rubbing shoulders with housewives, celebrities pushing against proles. And every pair of eyes will be drinking in the details, absorbing every nuance. Recording the memory for playback.*

*Then it will happen.*

*A crumpled twenty will be thrown from the circle. Cindy will look up, her eyes picking out the fat, red-haired man who threw the money. Other heads will turn, their focus shifting, watching as the purple note lands among the blood, puke, piss and shit. And like the first stone of a rockslide, it will loosen others.*

*Chain-reaction.*

*Reaching into pockets, wallets and purses, they will fill their hands. And with silent, reverent expectation they will throw their money at Cindy's feet. The notes will drift onto the fluid slick concrete or land on the fallen victim;*

*tens, twenties, and more. And then the voices will rise again. They'll grow in volume and insistence. Baying for blood. For death.*

*Cindy will look at the scattering of notes, knowing by their quantity and denomination that they've paid in full. But the final decision won't be hers to make. She will raise her eyes, scanning the crowd, searching. And then she'll see the hulking man-shape, standing in an oasis of calm.*

*He will nod.*

*And now she'll play her part. Ignoring the pain that has replaced the adrenalin, she'll stride across the tightening circle, careless of where she stands. Cash, gummed with coagulated blood, will be sticking to the soles of her boots.*

*She'll reach the woman, rolling her from a foetal position, till she's lying on her back. Cindy will straddle her. The ex-policewoman will look at her through the broken mask of her face. A face that had been little more than average. She'll mumble and raise her arms in a pitiable defence. Cindy will push aside these pathetic, reaching hands and grab first one fistful of matted hair, then another.*

*Cindy will smash the woman's head into the concrete floor. Spak.*

*Spak.*

*Spak.*

*Spak.*

*All the while, the roars, screams and yells of the crowd; their individual voices obliterated in the verbal melee. The sight and smell, the knowledge that what they see is real will be driving them to ecstatic howls. Primal, palpable and, above all, honest.*

*But then it will be over. The dead woman's head smashed open like an egg, grey matter mashed and stuck among the tangled mess of her hair.*

*Climax achieved, the emotions will grow stale, already being replaced by guilt and embarrassment.*

*Cindy will wipe her hands on the corpse's t-shirt and stand, starting to gather the scattered money.*

The waitress appears, carrying a plate and fork. On the plate, drenched in thick dark syrup and dusted with near black cocoa is a deep, wide wedge of chocolate cake. Three layers of light sponge, each cemented to the other with rich chocolate icing and with more of the same icing spread over its surfaces.

Cindy's eyes light up with childlike delight as it's placed before her. "Perfect," she tells the waitress.

"Hope you enjoy it, kid," the waitress says, with a smile. "Just looking at it's put ten pounds on my rear end."

Cindy smiles in response to the waitress's comments, then picks up the fork, cutting deep into the cake and lifting a mouthful to her lips. "It doesn't get much better than this."

## Wallpaper

Catherine Baird

She puts pictures of wolves and waterfalls on her computer
Screensavers
She wishes someone would notice
when she has gone off for a panini
Someone
who could see deep into her wild heart
via her desktop display
She waits for someone to say Wow!
That is a beautiful picture
now I see that you too must be beautiful
Inside
Under
Within
Deep down
Truly madly etc
She wishes.

# Comfortably Numb

Eddie McGonnell

Your perfume hung in the air
Like some invitation to amour.
Helloes were exchanged as you laid down
The obligatory bottle of wine,
And the awkward moment was broken
By the nectar of Pink Floyd
Singing through the sentiment of time.
We talked the language of trivia,
Each verbally sparring for that opening
Which would allow us to declare our intentions.
My mind hopped across the barbed wire
Of true confession,
As I longed to tell you
My secret.
Love stalked our conversation,
But could not find an opening.
My glass of wine felt as if it were lubricating
The words I really did not wish to say,
As you talked about
T in the Park and Johnny Depp and Gucci handbags.
While I edged ever nearer
Towards the precipice of emotional suicide.

The first few words of sombre revelation
Stopped you from making that first kiss,
The prelude to our love-pact
Which my illness-ravaged body
Could not possibly fulfil.
I watched your eyes as I bared my soul
And drowned in the blueness
Of your unremitting pain.
The ordinary things seem less ordinary.
And this doesn't seem the time to play the hero.
Can you tell me;
Will our love survive?
Until you do,
I am,
Comfortably numb.

# 2pm

Danny O'Connor

I hate that; when you finally waken up and your eyes are plastered together so tight that you can't tell if it's day or night. You don't have the energy left to tear one eyelid away from the other. Your eyeballs are stuck in some grit- filled trench at the bottom of their sockets and they can't scope the terrain.

Thankfully your hearing's ok. She's getting her revenge in all right. The washing machine's spinning like a drug-crazed dervish. The hoover hasn't lost its jet-engine whine and the food processor's grinding its way through enough root vegetables to feed the French.

Yes, it's those little somethings along with the desert-parched throat, the combination of stale sweat and even staler urine that hint to you that all is not well in your particular patch of the Garden of Eden.

Getting up's an effort too far. You grope blindly at the bedside cabinet for your fags. Your outstretched thumb brushes against cold glass and an empty vodka bottle clunks to the floor and spins across the linoleum expanse between you and the door. It's funny how the fall of an empty vodka bottle is the easiest of the day-after sounds to detect.

You stop groping for your fags because you remember that you quit smoking years ago. But, if that's the case then how come your mouth tastes like the inside of a battered old ashtray?

. You can feel it in your bones that it's going to be one of those days. No-one will be talking to you to start with. She'll shield the left side of her face from you, unwilling to award you the reassurance of seeing the bruises. The oldest will have been packed off to his gran's at first light and told not to play with knives. The youngest will just ignore you: like yesterday, and the day before yesterday, and all the tomorrows to come.

Then once you've downed a cup of tea and puked it back up again and stayed in the toilet for a good hard shite, the recriminations will start. Once upon a time there was a variation to these recriminations but these days the litanies have a sameness about them. A boringness even. But all these lectures for your own good, these hectorings, they all come down to the one thing. You've let the beast, the monster that is the real you, out again. The you that you used to be, the one she fell in love with; him, he fucked-off long ago.

There's no point in going round to your mother's to scrounge the price of a hair-of-the-dog. She'll just see you in your decrepitude, smile that little secret smile of hers and tell you that you're just like your da.

That's it maw; crucify me with pity.

# No One Gets Hurt

Craig Murray

No one gets hurt
We got together to use each other
Your perfect skin, soft to the touch
Lures me back for more
There's no love, only lust
Anything more means too much
I want something I can walk away from easily.

# A Negative Statement

Eddie McGonnell

Oblivion is just a needle away
And escape beckons like an irresistible dream
It is difficult to hear life's dark murmurs
When one is probing the mind-blowing experience
Of physical and mental euphoria.
A negative statement is being prepared
And a young mind will be transported
Down the labyrinthine hell
Of drugs dependency,
While
A small voice goes unheeded,
As selfishness rotates within our midst
And the seeds of self-destruction
Are sown within an awful indifference.
The old men will tell stories
Of a society which died
Not because of war or pestilence,
But because hope foundered
On the hedonistic values of self-pleasure

# Hunger

Danny O'Connor

Hunger, there is only hunger. The hunger came first. Before I knew I was me, I was gnawed at by the terrible hunger. I am consumed by this hunger and it won't go away.

I have only the knowledge of myself. There is nothing else in my universe. I hear my heartbeat and I feel my puny muscles swim, but only the hunger seems real.

The hunger came first. Then, through the umbilical cord, I was Smacked, I was Horsed, I was Charlied and I was super-alive. I could fly to unknown heights, I could dive to unknown depths and I could commune with the cosmos. I understood all, I felt all, I knew all. Then there was nothing.

Into this void rushed the hunger. It filled every nook, every cranny, every corner of my omniverse.

I fought to fill the hunger. My toothless mouth sought to tear, my nail-less fingers sought to claw and my feet kicked. The birth-canal was too long a route to take. I was in a hurry to feed the hunger. The shortest way was straight through the stomach wall.

Thus did I tear from my mother's womb. Now I lie, after taking my first scabrous breaths, in this artificial womb. My eyes are bandaged against the harsh neon light and a needle-drip is stabbed at my left heel. The counterfeit methadone is pumped into my screaming veins to quell my thrashing limbs. I know now the deceit of man. I yell for my Smack. I scream for my Horse. I roar for my Charlie. No solace comes. The counterfeit can never feed the hunger that gnaws at what I now know to be my soul.

I lie abandoned by the mother who never wanted me. My limbs are too weak to lift my head from the floor of the incubator. I shit and pee in fear that the hunger will never be filled and my heart learns rage.

All I see is a vista of meaningless tomorrows where the hunger never leaves me. This knowledge dragoons hate to the fore.

I hate me.

I hate having being born.

I hate the world, for the world will not feed my hunger.

A new thought springs from the torrid depths of my soul.

Revenge.

I will be revenged.

The world will know my revenge.

The methadone piped to my heart hails a brief lessening in my torment with its sour siren call.

If I am tortured by the world, in my revenge I will torture the world. Then the world on fire will heat the cold hunger of my being.

A second thought occurs. There are those who Smacked, who Horsed, who Charlied my mother. I will seek them out. I will be their slave. I will be their pet, their toy, their plaything and in return they will Smack, will Horse, will Charlie me.

Slavery and revenge: revenge and slavery. My life will cannon from one to the other and back again. I will be a metaphysical pinball between these pillars and sear my soul on a diet of heroin and hate.

My slavery is real. I will be a twenty-first century slave. I will be a modern slave, a high-tech slave. I will take my beatings. I will take my rapes and I will smile at my masters' bidding.

I will prey on the old, the infirm, and the weak. I will show only the mercy I have been shown. For I am the whirlwind reaped on an uncaring world, a world whose booty will be mine.

I will take my portion and I will fill my veins, killing each as I inject the needle. My arms, my legs, my groin; anywhere a vein can be slapped up as a golden pathway connecting me and the heroin, my soul's desire.

My soul's desire: once Smacked; once Horsed; once Charlied, I am omnipotent in my omniverse. My right hand is Pestilence and my left hand is Death.

# Crystal Voices

Hugh Reynolds

Melanie shook her hands in the water to agitate the liquid soap in order to wash the dishes left after dinner. She liked to stand at the sink and watch her daughter play in the garden; it took away the boredom of the chore. 'It'll soon be Christmas, happy times', muttered Melanie to no-one but herself.

Her daughter, Megan, loved the garden; it was her own little world. The electric wheelchair that she sat in let her move about the whole area. An area designed and built by her father. He had made it in such a way as to encompass every separate section with different types of bushes, plants and shrubs. His greatest triumph was the wide pathway that twisted and turned this way and that with small undulating hillocks that allowed Megan to experience the outdoor area despite her limited mobility. When she did this at speed she giggled and squealed with delight, much to the great pleasure of her parents.

A pair of arms slipped around Melanie's waist. "I see she's talking to the fairies again", said Alex.

"They're not fairies," replied Melanie "They are crystal voices!"

"Oh excuse me," said Alex nuzzling his wife's ear as she snuggled into his grasp.

"That is the last light you know", Alex said as he pointed to the one remaining foot high light that still carried illumination. Once there were as many as ten multi-coloured lights in the garden, but it seemed that every night over the last couple of weeks a different light had gone out. "I'll have to replace the lot. They only last so long these solar lights." He sighed, frustrated at not having had the time to replace those terminals which were now just dark shadows amongst the varied foliage of his daughter's leafy sanctuary.

Melanie wriggled free as she spoke, "Megan says she won't need new ones because the crystal voices say so!"

They turned and looked out of the window at their lovely girl, talking to, and laughing with, a solar garden light as if she could understand its every word. Sadness crept over them. She was a picture of happiness despite her disability. She had never walked and even after all this time the doctors were unable to diagnose her condition. The only thing they were certain of was that she would never be able to support herself for long enough to enable her to walk any meaningful distance. They hoped that one day she'd be able to stand and bear weight, at least.

Melanie had finished the dishes and Alex was reading his paper while in the background *A Christmas Carol,* a staple diet of Christmas Eve television, blared out unwatched. Just then the door opened and in came Megan in her usual cautious manner, careful not to bump into the furniture or the six foot Christmas tree that took pride of place in the small but homely living area. Her face glowed with either the fresh air or the excitement of Christmas Eve, or both.

"The last crystal voice has invited you both to watch it leave!" Megan's voice was a pitch higher than usual as if to hold back a secret.

"Okay," said her dad as he stood. From the kitchen window they watched the light as it began to dim. Just as Megan predicted, and just has she had done on previous nights.

"Aw, it's losing power," said Melanie, a little confused as to how her daughter knew this was going to happen again.

"That's alright!" exclaimed Megan, "It said that it would be like that at first."

"Now it's gone completely", said Alex regretfully. It would be a couple of days before he'd be able to get to the garden centre for replacements. Although his saving grace was that he hoped Megan would be too engrossed in her gifts to worry about the garden for a few days.

Melanie and Alex both stared out into Megan's garden, the melancholy of the moment not lost on them. It was with a start that they felt simultaneous taps on their backs. In unison they turned from the window to see their daughter s*tanding* before them.

"It's a gift from the crystal voices!" exclaimed an excited Megan as tears welled-up in her parents' eyes.

"2009 will be a Crystal Christmas", cried Melanie and Alex.

# Money, Money, Money

Erin McHugh

When I was wee I got coppers for the van and I thought I was rich,
Now I throw my coppers away,
I ask my mum why she is rolling in it,
She says she saves her coppers up every day

## An Accident

William N. Dyer

I was with my mother. She would take me, every day, to New City Road to do the shopping. It was like that then. Anything perishable would be bought on the day it would be used. We didn't have a fridge.

As we came to the road we heard an enormous bang, followed by lots of scraping and crunching sounds. Pandemonium breaking loose, as my mother would say later, when she came to relate the tale to my granny.

"Mammy, Mammy, what's all that noise?"

"There's just been an accident in the road."

I rushed forward almost slipping away from my mother. "Jean, don't you dare run away from me." She strengthened her grasp on my hand.

"I want to see what's going on."

"It's not for little girls' amusement. Someone might be hurt."

"What's that wailing sound, Mammy?"

"It's the ambulance and the police to fix things."

"What things, Mammy?" I asked as I tried to squirm to the front of the onlookers.

"There might be people hurt in the cars. The police

will want to know what happened."

I pulled my mother forward in my attempt to gain a good view. We edged towards the accident.

From behind I heard a scream. I twisted to see who had made that horrible noise. I was showered by a warm fountain of my mother's breakfast as I completed the turn.

The sight must have been horrendous to have evoked such a response. My mother whisked us both home. She never said a word about the incident in my presence, ever.

It took only till that evening for me to find the cause of my mother's gross reaction. While I was at the swings in the Phoenix Park Wee John came by.

"Jean?"

"Hello, Wee John."

"Have you no heard about Davie MacCumming?"

"He's no been lifted by the polis again?"

"No, you've no heard?"

"What are you up to, Wee John?"

"I'm no up to anything."

"Well?", I said in my most teacher like voice and waited.

"I thought everyone knew."

"Knows what?"

"Davie was killed in an accident this morning. His head was chopped off. In one piece. That's what ma da said anyway."

"You're having me on. Ma Mammy and me were there this morning; and ma Mammy would have told me what had happened."

It was only then that the truth came to me. My mother's reaction and her silence about what she had seen. I ran home, my mind emptied of any meaning. Why had she not told me?

When I got to our door I pounded it relentlessly and shouted for ma Mammy. My granny opened the door.

"Wheest, wheest lassie. Come with me."

"I want to see my Mammy."

"Now's no a good time. She's hurtin' just like you, my wee Jeannie. She saw something terrible and it's upset her."

"Bit it wisnae me Granny."

"A know, but yir ma canna stand the thought o' some poor mither being without hir wee boy the nicht. She's fair hert broken."

Years later I realised how strong my mother had been that day; in spite of what she had seen, she still let me out on my own to play with my friends.

## 'Ministry of Truth'

J. B. Quinn

Terror Alert
Terror attack
They're everywhere; watch your back
From the South
And to the East
Creating war, destroying peace
Send in the troops
Helping hands
Exchanging 'democracy' for foreign lands
Marching bands
Lead the way
Jingoistic crusaders on display
Might is right
Gather the forces
Protecting interests, pillaging resources
Our way or the highway
Trample dissent underfoot
Crush the rights of others with a new jackboot
Body count
Collateral damage
Humanity subtracted, multiply the carnage
Stockpile lies

Corrupt the truth
Deception hides behind every bush
Appearances mislead
It's all an act
Orwell's 'Ministry of Truth' is back.

## Something Lacking

Danny O'Connor

I know there's something lacking
To my moral fibre, there's no backing
It's God's returns queue for me
                                        I fear
You'll come over to see
                                        My tear
As it runs down my face
At my disgrace

# Old Yellow Bricks

James A. Stewart

It is with heavy heart I replay this tale of woe. The Emerald City has been lost; and all of Oz will soon follow. The grandeur of its bright green structures and cosmopolitan clientèle has been torn asunder by an evil incarnate. Eternal darkness has descended on us. At the heart of this devilish dawning is a power so strong, so malignant and so callous that to meet it is to meet one's maker.

Our journey began immediately after the Winter Equinox. We were sitting by the fire in the village bar when we received a communication from Dorothy. She had been incarcerated in the witches' haven in the Emerald City. Luck was to befriend her and she managed to make convivial acquaintance with one of the garish brood of flying monkeys, and through sympathetic influencing, Dorothy persuaded this ghastly beast to deliver us a message. How could we refuse after everything this sweet little girl had done for us? I had her to thank for my brains, Lion owed her his courage, and how he would need this; and the Tin Man's heart sunk when he read her note to us. Included with the note was her petite blue and white checked bow. We were compelled into action.

On the road, old yellow bricks were fighting a losing battle with weeds. All over the main drag to the city there were lumps and bumps brought about by the weeds' little victories. Some sections had been plundered of all their surface materials as scavengers fled with the blocks for some unknown purpose. The possibilities for the use of the bricks were infinite, but in the now unsafe Oz it was almost certain weaponry would be the most likely employment to which the former iconic road would be put.

I shuddered as I pictured a yellow brick covered in thick red blood. It was a vision to which I awoke daily, but one which was now entering my awakened consciousness time and again. It could be no coincidence that as we neared the Emerald City my head began to hurt evermore and the visions became more graphic and disquieting. I should have understood this warning.

We travelled on foot, the three of us plus the exhausted messenger, and we proceeded with no small amount of caution. We spoke little on the first day, uneasy excitement grated against our nerves. Lion found his newly acquired courage was being tested to the full, but I was able to control his fears through rational wiles. Tin Man was very emotional; we had to persuade him to persist with our quest on more than one occasion.

We carried the fatigued monkey for the first day and stopped only for sustenance. Dorothy's note smacked of desperation. She asked for me to lead the expedition. She was sure with my cerebral authority I would soon construct a plan which would free her from the dungeon in which she was being held.

We walked for two days further; rain drenched us and I must acknowledge, dampened our spirits. All around us it appeared the sky was blue, yet one constant cloud drenched us head to toe, morning to night; even when we took a diversion athwart the Munchkin fields the rain followed. Without oil, I was fretful about Tin Man's ability to motor on. I suggested we take refuge from the torrent in a nearby homestead. Tin Man had to be persuaded to take this reprieve from the downpour; my valiant friend was jumping between fear of the possible outcomes of the mission to us and the need to aid a friend.

We reached the dilapidated looking outbuilding as twilight was setting. The menace of the darkening atmosphere was nary more plain than on the road to the Emerald City at this time, and while we had been relatively unmolested on our expedition thus far, the bloody bawls that came from inside the farmhouse astride the barn in which we wished to seek refuge gave us a stark reminder of the danger all around.

In all Ozian history I had never heard such a guttural wailing. We three cowered for all our wretched lives were worth; our winged-monkey companion escaped into the rafters and hid. True to form our brave friend Lion made the first motion to establish what in the name of the Wizard was happening.

"We must save that poor soul." he whispered. Even in the murky half-light of the dank barn, I could see his teeth exposed in menace. Not to me or Tin Man, but to the foe unknown next door.

"Did you hear the terror in the scream?" asked Tin Man, "It has sent my cogs whirling in protest. Whoever is in there is dead already, and we'd be next to join that unfortunate one if we are foolish enough to reveal ourselves here. Stay put."

"No." said Lion. "We must help. Dorothy made sacrifices to win my courage for me, and I am not about to defame her efforts by hiding in a stinking barn while someone is killed."

I was about to step between my quarrelling companions when a second scream filled our ears. This was a different scream. There was no fear in it, only pleasure. Thunder clapped in the air and as the lightning crashed, silhouetted through the barn's skylight was the unmistakable outline of a witch on her broom. The evil presence sped off toward the city. This ended the discourse between Lion and Tin Man. I felt there may be some information of value in the house which could help us in our quest.

"Let's go in." I said.

We waited a few minutes before venturing into the ordinary looking farmhouse. Ordinary in appearance perhaps; but the shrieks and cowls had put us on edge. The building's façade was typical of rural Ozian architecture. The entrance was around four feet tall. It was large for a Munchkin construction, and whilst there were two storeys, only the ground level had windows. The dark sky, brightened by intermittent and now distant lightning bursts, gave this commonplace building a sinister feel. Even the normally indefatigable valour of Lion wavered as we approached.

I entered first, with Tin Man next and Lion keeping the rear should we find ourselves ambushed from behind. There were two rooms on the lower level, a kitchen with a pantry door and what appeared to be a sitting room, though impossible to determine definitively due to the disorder of the furniture strewn room – it looked as it there had been a massive trashing of this room but like the others it was empty of people. We then moved upstairs, keeping the same formation as before. Every creak of the vacillating stairwell was analogous to a spear in my midriff, but I steadied my resolve and used the noises as a catalyst to expedite my ascension. Lion and Tin Man followed close behind.

At the top, there were three doors, two to our left but there was no need for us to consider the contents therein as a low moaning noise came from behind the warped looking door to our right. With exaggerated vigilance I led the way to the chamber. Inside was the most horrific scene. Tin Man fainted and the clatter of his metallic frame on the hard wood floor startled me, and brought our attention to the Munchkin who had been nailed to the far wall. The poor fellow was attached to the wall so as to make his body into a star shape. Blood dripped from the wounds in his feet and hands, and the bruises from his beating were already evident on his naked body. Through the bruises I could make out the features of Pieter, an amiable Munchkin and friend of Dorothy's from her previous visit. He had been missing for nearly a week.

Slowly, I helped him down from his binds. I ordered Lion to get some water and to search for medical supplies in the kitchen. Alas, there was no medicine; only water and a rather contaminated looking towel were brought back. Pieter tried to speak but lapsed into unconsciousness; in which I could only imagine what horrible images were being played out. His groaning and sporadic spasms were suggestive of an altogether horrid series of dreams.

I cleaned his wounds as best as the scant resources would allow. Lion had to replenish the water supplies more than once. Tin Man was awake, but still not wholly recovered from his blackout. Pieter opened his left eye; the right was closed from heavy bruising.

"She was here...," he mumbled, coughing up blood and phlegm as he wrestled with the next line, "...run for your lives."

"Who was here?" Tin Man asked, "We saw the witch leaving earlier."

"The Wicked Witch was here."

"Which one? Dorothy killed the East and West witches." said Lion. Tin Man gulped.

"She who wants to reign supreme..." Before he could finish, Pieter fell back into darkness. Unlike his previous blackout there was no movement. A check on his pulse confirmed why.

"A Supreme Witch! This is dreadful, if she fulfils the prophecy, Oz will be subject to her dark rule for millennia." said Tin Man. This was indeed a dark day.

"What prophecy?" asked Lion.

I replied, "Ozian legend states when all four Oz witches are slain, a new, supreme witch will rise to have overall control of malignant magic in Oz. L. Frank Baum's *A History of Oz: Myths and Magic On the Yellow Brick Road* speculates the grasping of power will be opportunistic. There is no definite timeframe; only that it would happen sometime between the thirteenth and eighteenth Dynastic periods. We are, I believe, in period sixteen."

"And how does the witch rise?" Lion asked.

"Well, she either has to kill the witches, or kill those who killed them." I replied, and my own words lashed my mind into action, "Which means, Dorothy... oh my Wizard!"

"What is it?" asked Lion.

Tin Man had caught up by this point. "It means the supreme witch will have to kill her to take power." His metal frame dropped a shade or two at the thought. "I think we should reconsider going to Emerald City." he said.

Lion and I replied in unison and with gusto. "No!"

We journeyed for two more days, but not before we buried unfortunate Pieter in a shallow cairn, as is Munchkin burial convention, a fact I picked up on when I inherited my new intellect. By now we had lost the winged-monkey and despite our constant ruminations none of us could find a feasible explanation for the murder of our Munchkin friend. Neither could we explain why he was in the farm where we found him. It looked like he had been there for days, and one can only speculate as to the horrors to which he was subjected during his incarceration.

"Why do you think he was in that farmhouse in the first place?" asked Tin Man, as we filtered back into a familiar topic.

"Perhaps he was seeking shelter, the same as us." Lion replied.

"I don't know. There is something not right in all of this. Pieter's home was in the Emerald City itself, why would he come two days out?" I said, and my companions could only look ahead in befuddlement.

This conversation cycled over and over again. By the time we reached the Emerald City we had regurgitated the same arguments innumerable times. The conclusion? We had no idea. Personally, I was finding it difficult to concentrate with the visions blinking through my mind almost hourly. I had these to cope with, as well as the mystery around Pieter's death, and of course, the mission to emancipate our treasured Dorothy. Even with my new brains I was under colossal strain.

It was approaching evening when we reached the Emerald City. The incessant raincloud was on our shoulders all the way. It stopped at once the minute we passed through the city gates. I noticed at once the difference in the atmosphere and the streets were practically deserted.

We looked up an old friend in the *Emerald Bar.* In his usual place sat Ulysses Gaginwold, the foremost authority on Ozian witchcraft and wizardry; he had learned from Baum himself. He greeted our entrance with a courteous nod of the head. Before we could reach him the barman stepped in between us.

"Travellers, huh? We've not had many out-of-towners for a while, but you boys are well known in these parts. Maybe it is best if you about foot and start your journey home now."

I was about to protest. Never had we been made so unwanted. Indeed, the barman and I had a great many topical debates after I secured my brains. They were the kind of discussions one could only hold with a barman. Before I began my protestations I noticed Ulysses nodding in agreement and perplexity hit me: I couldn't comprehend. The barman pushed us back out of the door and into night air, but not before secreting a note in the straw of my neck.

I guided Lion and Tin Man to a quiet corner and we read his note; I replay it verbatim here so as to allow you the reader to appreciate its contents:

*Go home now!*
*Dorothy is already gone.*
*You must save yourselves, and us.*
*UG*

"Do you think it is a riddle?" I asked. Tin Man and Lion were perplexed. The handwriting suggested it had been scrawled in haste, and with Ulysses' initials, it was clear he penned the message.

It was time to seek shelter and regroup. My head was pounding from visions. Tin Man was looking exhausted and, since we found Pieter, he had been rather recalcitrant in conversation. A good night's sleep was what he needed. Lion arranged to take first watch as we sought respite from the biting cold in the trees that border the grounds of the university. The grand old establishment had been closed for a few weeks, but like all of the Emerald City, it gave the impression of being careworn from years of disregard. It was hard to reconcile in one's mind the fact that this place had throbbed with enthusiastic students less than one month earlier.

During my watch, I peered out over the Emerald City. In what seemed like less than no time it had turned from a thriving metropolis into a place which reeked of sadness and apathy. The sheen from the emerald edifices was gone, replaced by a veneer of scum. The pinpoint architecture, once mathematically perfect, gave the impression it was closing in on itself. The buildings looked closer than I remembered, and the gaps between the rooftops appeared narrower than those at ground level, as if the multi-storeys in the business district were leaning toward their across-road neighbours. Scraggy animals roved the streets at night and the carnival ambiance of the city was lost. If I had tear ducts, I would have cried there and then.

Somehow I had drifted off to sleep as I leaned against an age-old tree. My dreams were infinitely lucid and of Dorothy, she was beseeching me to join her. She preached about there not being a middle anymore. A middle what? I asked her. She told me I would know when the time was right.

I awoke in the morning more confused than ever. Tin Man and Lion were sleeping thoroughly as I watched daybreak's first light shine over the Emerald City. Even in the period in which I was in dreamland it seemed the city had aged. Rooftops were starting to sprout foliage and the muted atmosphere of the preceding evening was carried over into the morning. The only sounds were of those trying to leave the city, and from our vantage point I could see the gates were closed.

It was almost time to wake my tranquil looking companions, a pair of bedrocks in a trying time, when I heard a rustle from the tree behind us. With prudence I approached the tree. Hanging by his tail on the first level of branches was our messenger friend; the winged-monkey. He had a new parchment. I examined it; the contents were astonishing. Dorothy knew we were here, perhaps our friend Ulysses had gotten a message to her. She instructed us to follow the monkey as he would be able to lead us into the witches' castle.

After a moment's refreshment - vital sustenance in our quest - we set off, scampering behind the fast moving escort and toward the highest building in the Emerald City. Through backstreets and alleyways we traversed until we came across a channel which was trickling only a small amount of wash into the lake below. To our fortune, the grill was corroded and we prised it off with great ease. We each squeezed through the small entrance which was somewhat of an illusion as inside the ceiling was some two metres high, and there was ample headroom for us to walk straight-backed down its length. At a junction our guide broke left, but directed us to go right. We walked for no more than two minutes in the miserable orifice, but it felt like an hour. I was aware we were on a gradual incline and speculated this was some sort of storm drain.

"Sshhh! Listen." said Lion, putting his paws up to hush us.

From above we could hear muffled voices. Ahead was a sliver of light and we made for its tantalising little glow. As soon as we neared the light, doors slammed around us. Above us a familiar screech filled the air. Moments later through some unknown and uncontrolled means all three of us passed out, and my last vision was of a blood encrusted yellow brick.

Some indefinite period later I came to. Beside me was Lion. In contrast to him, I was not tethered and bound. Our prison was a simple cube, three paces by three paces and probably three paces high as well. It was a sterile room of granite. I could envisage people dying here.

The door to the cell opened. A haggard goblin beckoned me forth. I followed him through a maze of dark corridors with only his meagre torch for illumination. I was sure I had passed my former holding cell at least twice – it was as if we were going around in circles. Before I plucked up the valour to protest we stepped through a grand oak door. The light momentarily blinded me; a mix of greens and yellows of all shades. My head began to throb with awful pain; I could see the yellow brick with all of its blood, only this time, I recognised the hand of its executor. It was me, the great and intelligent Scarecrow.

A searing pain came across the back of my thighs. I bent over and onto my knees. "Kneel before the Supreme Witch." growled the goblin.

I looked up, and to my astonishment Dorothy was sitting upon a throne of gold encrusted with precious gems.

To her right was Tin Man, hung by his wrists above a vat of molten metal. Such was the heat that I could feel it from where I was across the room. Tin Man was conscious but gagged. The trepidation in his eyes was palpable. He had been crying oil as the black lines from his eyes testified.

"Hello, Strawman."

"What's going on, Dorothy?"

Dorothy's evil tone shocked me as she told me how she needed us to come to her and allow her to complete her transformation into the Supreme Witch. Pieter had told her when someone kills a witch they inherit her powers and only a female can use them to their full potential. She boasted about how she had already killed the witches from the North, South and West: and now had only one more to go.

My head was gyrating in mixed up leaps and bounds; dear Dorothy was in fact a witch and a mass murderer. Something about her chronicle didn't fit. She could see my confusion, and ergo, and in keeping with her new self, she taunted me.

"Come on, Scarecrow. Where is the hole in my tale? Use your brains."

Her goading sparked my intellect into life and immediately. "Wait. You killed the Wicked Witch of the East when you first came here," I reasoned out aloud, "and then you killed the Wicked Witch of the West to secure your return home. You say you have killed the Witches of the North and South. The set must be complete. If so, then why this charade?"

"Ask your friend." she said as the goblin removed the gag from Tin Man's mouth.

"I'm sorry, old friend. I should have told you." was all Tin Man could say.

"I don't understand..."

"Of course you don't." cackled Dorothy. "Neither did I until I tortured Pieter to find out. You see, when I killed the West Witch, I felt her power transfer to me. It was a wonderful sensation. I embraced the malignant side of the power, lest it destroy me and drive me to suicide...."

"This can't be true." I interrupted.

"Save it, Scarecrow. What confused me was why this sensation never came to me when I killed the East Witch. From my discussions with Pieter, who was first on the scene when I arrived from Kansas, I concluded someone else had killed her before I got there. I got the credit but someone else had already gotten the power."

Pausing for effect, Dorothy stared me down as if I should know what was coming next.

"Oh, come on, Brains. Work it out! Tin Man killed the Wicked Witch of the East."

Dumbfounded, I replied, "How?"

"Tell him, Tin Man, before I melt you and complete my destiny."

Tin Man looked me in the eyes, my head throbbed. Visions of blood splattered yellow bricks came to me. This time, the hand was metallic. In my mind I saw him beat the witch with a brick from behind. He hit her once, twice and then she grabbed him and he started to rust and seize up, I could see the fear in his eyes as if I were watching a movie. Then the witch let him go and stared at the sky mouth agape. Taking advantage, Tin Man gave her an almighty clout with the brick. Her eyes closed immediately and in a fraction of a second Tin Man was propelled away from the witch; in his place stood a farmhouse from Kansas. He looked at me, oil streaming from his eyes.

"The Munchkins hired me to kill the witch", he said, "And Pieter was on hand to ensure I completed the job. I had no heart, I didn't care about life. I was a professional assassin. After my experience with the witch I wanted to die."

"Why didn't you just tell us?" I asked.

"I didn't understand the power and could only embrace two elements: telepathy and cloud control. I tried to use both to put you off," he said in a soft whimper. "I was scared I'd lose you and Lion. You're the only friends I have. This heart has cost me more than it has given. I am impotent in the face of emotion...", he was interrupted by Dorothy's demented crowing.

"Scarecrow, the arrogance of your superior knowledge brought about by your 'bran-new' brains meant you couldn't see the danger signals." Dorothy sneered, "You ignored his hints and subtle pleas, the fear, the cloud when he tried to debilitate himself, just as I knew you would."

"How can you be so cocksure?" I snarled.

"Because I gave you your brains and I gave Tin Man his heart. I knew he couldn't pull out no matter how much he tried; he needed you to stop him. But I gave you a massive blind spot where your rationality should be, and your arrogance placed you in the role of murderer, which you will get a chance at, I promise." Dorothy paused but only to let me realise my own folly. "You misread Ulysses' attempts to stop your trio of would-be-emancipators; and he's been dealt with for his insubordination."

Dorothy's stare impaled me and the malevolence of her speech cut through me. Dear Ulysses dead! But this shrivelled into insignificance when I considered her observations about converting me to a murderer. She smiled and the inside of my head exploded into a raging inferno, I felt as though flames were coming out of my eyes, nostrils and mouth. I screamed and fell backwards and writhed around the ground in endless circles. I have no organs, but the area where an ordinary person's intestines would be bubbled as if they were lava from a spewing volcano.

Then all of a sudden it stopped. I opened my eyes and Dorothy's face was impassive, she looked to her left, I followed, and where Tin Man once hung was an empty space. She laughed long and loud and my ears shrieked in protest as my brain reverberated around my patchwork cranium.

"Are you ready to commit murder?" she asked, "I believe you are."

"Never!" I screamed.

"If you don't I will put you through the fire you have just experienced every hour on the hour for the rest of your miserable life. And I will ensure your life is very long... you will kill Lion for me. He is trussed in his cell as you know."

"Never!" I cried again but in my head I had visions of a yellow brick and splattered blood. I could see a lion's mane and a handmade of straw.

"You will kill him."

I protested once more. The prophecy returned in my head, and in my heart I knew despite my protestations, Dorothy was right. The middle ground between good and evil had vanished; it was time to pick sides. Dorothy may have played me sweet with the weak points from my now-not-so-superior-brains, but I was smart enough to know which team to side with.

# Rummy's Remedy

J. B. Quinn

R
o
l
l
u
p
Roll up, roll up
Buy before you try
Rummy's snake-oil cure
A profitable potion for every nation
May cause nausea; inducing dehydration
Roll up, roll up
Buy before you try
Rummy's snake-oil cure
A multinational very cold remedy
Brought to you by Shock Therapy.

# Deep Sea Death

Danny O'Connor

Who would have thought, even a week ago, that the human race would be pitched against a microscopic beastie only ten microns tall, and that the winner would inherit the earth and the loser cease to exist? That's right: it's turned out to be evolution versus extinction, a matter of life and death.

In the red corner is us: all corpuscles, tools and lateral thinking. In the blue corner is as small a beastie as you can imagine. Unambitious, unchanged and unloved for millions upon millions of years.

Until the day it touched the hand of man, less than a week ago, it swam the bottom reaches of the ocean for three hundred and thirty-three million years. It had its own niche in the microscopic food-chain, the top of which, in its turn, fed the krill. The number and proliferation of its predators set the limits to its individual lifespan and its numbers.

Untimed millennia ago a spontaneous mutation occurred. Exponential growth meant a strong colony of these mutants established a toehold on life. Traditional predators soon learned that to eat them was to invoke their own death, and so concentrated on feeding on their un-mutated cousins instead.

With no natural predators, the colony grew only as large as its own level of foodstock allowed. And so the mutants reached a symbiosis with their environment which did not preclude a spot of cannibalism on their cousins in times of extremity.

Millions of years passed in this tranquillity of stasis. Until one day Mother Earth threw herself into a tumult and a tsunami, caused by the emergence of a seamount or sea-floor volcano, passed through the mutant colony. The survivors were washed through millions of square kilometres of ocean-bed. They did what the victims of all diaspora do: they got on with the business of living. Some colonies failed, others migrated to more favourable conditions for life. More millennia passed and there were now sufficient numbers of mutants in sufficiently diverse locations for them to require cataloguing as a separate sub-genus from their originator cousins.

Man knew nothing of this microscopic beastie until serious scientific study of the ocean-bed began as a prelude to underwater agriculture or aquagriculture, if you will. These aquagriculturalists saw themselves as the cutting-edge of technology and the saviours of mankind. As such, they thought of themselves as New Age alchemists enjoined in the search for inexpensive proteins as their new philosopher's stone. They were, therefore, driven and hungry for the mouth-watering milestones of success.

Our microscopic beastie remained hidden for the first thirty-odd years of the new scientific discipline of aquagriculture. That is, until some bright-spark searching for a PhD. thesis decided to decrease the gradation of mesh size of the net of the ocean-bed remote trawler. With this new illumination, the once thought sterile environment of the ocean-bed showed itself to be teeming with new and unknown forms of life. The next two generations of eager students looking for subject matter for their doctorates spent useful and productive careers cataloguing the varied microscopic species of the ocean-bottom. But none found the philosopher's stone of cheap protein to feed the burgeoning numbers of our hungry.

Still our beastie evaded the net of the cataloguers. It was not until this particular area of ocean investigation seemed all fished out for potential doctoral theses that a Jenny-come-lately, with a particularly methodical frame of mind hit upon the double trawl-net idea. Breathtakingly elegant in its simplicity, it re-revolutionised this area of research and it was bonanza time again for academic glories.

The basis of this second academic Yukon was, firstly a trawl-net whose mesh accorded with the smallest known specimen sizes and then, further down the shaft, a second net with an as yet unheard-of fineness of mesh. This double net at the point-of-trawl was significant due to the fact that humans and deep-ocean marine animals live in two entirely different environments. I am not talking about us living on land and breathing air and them living in the ocean and extracting oxygen from water. No, I refer of course, to atmospheric pressure. Just as any 'deep'-sea diver, who incidentally, only descends in tens of metres and has to be careful not to come up too soon or he would get the 'bends' (wherein a build-up of nitrogen would inflate his veins to bursting point); so too would a fish or any other creature used to an environmental pressure to the value of three atmospheres, explode well before reaching the surface and the one atmosphere of atmospheric pressure we inhabit.

All these generations of scientists had been cataloguing and working with microscopic cadavers. Moreover cadavers blasted with the changes in atmospheric pressure resulting in casualties mutilated as thoroughly as with a direct hit of TNT. Therefore the really small microscopic organisms fished up in the trawl were hidden amongst the detritus of blown-off limbs and viscera of larger animals caught in the same net. What the two-net method did was to keep all the bigger, known about, and boring previously recorded stuff, behind one mesh and allowed the smaller, scientifically unknown, and therefore sexy trawl to be collected in its own chamber.

Yet another generation of students, standing on the shoulders of these intellectual giants, searching for subject matter fit for a thesis, designed a collecting device which inserted a metal plate just below the larger trawl-net just prior to lifting the device to the surface.

As different animals have different skeletal structures and different morphology, they explode into oblivion at different depths on the journey to the surface. It would be left to a future generation of scientist, if we had one, to gain academic fame by applying a DVD-recorder to the device to record the sight of the pop-popping of marine animal cadavers and plot their depths of demise in a mortality-graph. No doubt the ensuing recording, set to a techno beat could become a chart-topper, going on to win the 'most artistically stunning' category industry video award.

Finally, after three hundred and thirty-three and-a-bit million years of peaceful, unknowing co-existence both our mutant and their fore-bear cousin are catalogued into the mind of man and, as reward, given double-barrelled Latin names with different endings to indicate both the proximity and yet difference in their genus. The different ending would incorporate the Latin term for the colour blue for the mutant and the exclusion of the Latin term for the colour blue for its denuded cousin.

It is here at the point of entering the catalogue of human knowledge that the whole story of this inedible, microscopic marine animal, found in only a relatively small area in the whole circumference of planet Earth's ocean-bed, should be concluded. It should have been left as a mere curiosity of a footnote in the science of aquamorphology.

Instead, the final horrific chapter could be laid at the honourable door of man's quest for scientific knowledge. Or, closer to truth, the less dignified barracuda scramble for academic recognition amongst its more voracious practitioners. No matter the motive. The fact was that mankind, represented by these 'cutting edge of technology' scientists decided to get to know this microscopic sea-creature after the aforementioned three hundred and thirty-three and-a-bit million years of peaceful, unknowing co-existence.

The starting point of the, ultimately suicidal, doctorate thesis of the latest aspirant to academic recognition was; and I paraphrase:

'Why does one genus of the wee beastie have a blue coloured sac in what we think is its gut, in an otherwise transparent skeleton, and the other genus have none?'

It was hoped that in answering this self-imposed question, the questioner would gain good standing in the academic world as well as permanent tenure in a minor university in one of the dust-bowl states. A commercial application found in answering the question was highly unlikely, but a none-the-less looked for by-product of the investigation. The satisfaction of pure scientific interest came quite far down the goal-orientated list of the modern aquagricultural scientist.

Our doctorate-seeking student provided the usual PhD. raft of endeavour on the subject matter. Attempts were made to plot the proliferation of both of the sub-genus. Guesstimates of relative numbers in different areas of the ocean bed were provided. Their relative positions in the microscopic food chain they inhabited were charted. All sorts of scientific endeavour was recorded. All of this academic padding was assiduously carried out but everyone knew that the nub of the subject was the blue sacs. What did the blue sac comprise of? What did it do? Or as any first year student of any 101 subject could parrot 'What is its structure and what is its function?' To get the answer to either of these questions you had to first get enough of the blue bits together in the one place to sample them. Various tests would have to be done to get a chemical analysis of the blue bits. Then, from that, the active ingredients would have to be deduced and all from an animal no bigger than ten microns tall. Still, in order to get a 'worthwhile' PhD., it would have to be done.

This is the point where some sloppiness in the scientific methodology crept in. In other circumstances it wouldn't have mattered but, this accident-waiting-to-happen, proved, in this instance to be fatal. You see it was all the fault of the very small quantities involved. For every gallon dredged along the ocean-bed only a thimbleful at most, would be of any use. Then only a microscopic amount of the blue sacs from the beastie could be harvested. Financial and time constraints led to a speeding-up of the procedures so that the turnaround time was shortened. This allowed another two 'missions' and two more thimbleful of the precious environment of the beastie to be harvested than if they had paid strict adherence to the safety protocols.

When the deadly event did occur, no one even noticed. This is what happened: The research assistant opening the collecting device and extracting the all-important thimbleful had taken off their protective gloves.

It was a warm day and carrying out the full process speedily was a demanding task; so one of the first things to go were the clumsy gloves which hindered the efficient opening of the device. It was only sea water after all, even if it did come from the deep ocean depths. It couldn't hurt anyone. No, the reason for the gloves was to prevent human contamination of the specimen; not to protect the human from the specimen. Anyway, in the rush to pull the sample from the device a mere teardrop of the precious thimbleful spilled on to the assistant's wrist.

The researcher didn't even feel the teardrop explode on to their wrist.

No one thought anything of it when the researcher called in with the cold and didn't leave their bunk for twenty-four hours.

In these competitive days everyone expected the researcher to return to work before they were fully fit.

No one was surprised when, one working day after exposure to the assistant that half the team called in with the cold.

The boat docked in harbour for the weekend. The crew went to party. The scientific high-fliers flew hither and thither to academic conferences.

It has been established that the incubation period in the host human is four days. The virus circled the globe in three.

Not one continent, one country, one city, town, village or hamlet has escaped.

No one even bothered to report the first researcher's death as being suspicious.

'Death by misadventure' is what it says on their death certificate. It is ironic that: 'Death by misadventure' is to be the final epitaph for the whole of mankind in just over a week from now.

That first researcher fell down dead-drunk at the crew party. The local M.E. only got suspicious when five cadavers with the same 'Alcoholic Poisoning' next day turned out to be from the same crew.

Two more days were wasted searching for non-existent illegal booze, with each suspect literally dying-off when confronted by the revenuers. It wasn't until some of these revenue-men themselves turned up seemingly drunk-to-death that the whistle was blown, revenuers being known for being an abstemious bunch.

It was, of course, too late by then. The whole world had caught this particular cold by now. It's only for the sake of scientific interest that I outline what can only be a putative guess at the morphology of the killer virus nicknamed 'deep-sea death' by our more frivolous tabloids.

That fatal teardrop of deep ocean water exploded onto the unnamed researcher's wrist and mingled with their sweat. The blue sac disintegrated on contact with the sweat enzymes which are not radically different from some genus of enzyme found in the gut. The enzymes in the sweat combined with the chemicals inside the sac to form a new compound.

This new chemical seeped deep into the sub-cutaneous tissue. Acting like a retro-virus, the active part of the enzyme invaded the vein walls and attached themselves to the platelets in the blood. Once there, they multiplied by the usual process of growth and division, like a cancer cell, although at a heightened rate, doubling themselves every time they passed through the aorta. The host, in this case, dealt with the perceived increase in alcohol level in the bloodstream as it usually did. It partied on and then passed out. By the time the level had become critically life-threatening four days of inebriation had passed. The normal water content in aspirated air from their breath had successfully mutated into an alcohol-rich water-seeking propellant ready to be breathed in by the next unsuspecting host.

Mankind has coexisted with alcohol since before the dawn of recorded time. But man has always been the active partner in the equation. His only response to alcoholic poisoning as an individual has been to either desist, or drink himself to death. Now for the first, and only time, mankind is the passive partner in an equation where water is literally being turned into wine. Unfortunately for man, he is ninety percent water and this philosopher's stone of an enzyme will not stop until it has had one over the eight. Eight pints of our blood, that is.

# The Last Few

James A. Stewart

A flurry of snow laced with the tell-tale sign of wasting falls lightly on the head of the last few, sheltering and shivering inside the near roofless burnt-out corpse of a centuries-old cottage.

Across the plains a faint orange glow recalls the carnage the last few pray that the glow's vendors are headed north, their prayers are interrupted, and denied, by the drone of a drone.

The last few jumble together under the scant canopy of their hiding place, praying silently for a miracle, redemption, emancipation; anything but the inevitable. A muffled cry from the last child born on Earth is stifled too late.

The drone's drone changes, it is no longer searching, it is closing in. The last few recognize silence's shield has been broken, they pray aloud, and above, the alien sky-vehicle's under carriage turns brilliant red in preparation.

Mankind's prayers are interrupted for the last time.

# Anthropomorphic

Alexander J. Cunningam

When you first see Rosie Harper's Golden Retriever, Harry, it's dressed in jeans and a t-shirt. It wanders into the living room of the suburban house, playing a handheld games console and muttering about losing a life. He has Nike trainers on his rear paws and stands close to four and a half feet in height.

He moves to the settee, watched by ten-year-old Rosie, and sits, leaning back, his eyes having never left the small screen.

"Harry," Rosie says, her voice commanding. "Off the furniture."

In a city centre executive high rise of glass and steel, Ben Kendal's cat, Galore, is just getting ready to go on her nightly prowl. She's dressed in the best of the latest feline fashion, but it's her jet-black fur and piercing eyes that set off the killer look.

"And behave yourself tonight, Gal," Ben grumbles to the two foot tall creature as it hovers near the door. "Don't go slummin' it with those alley cats again or it'll be off to the vets for you."

Galore regards Ben with a dismissive glance as she slides out the door.

And in an East End tenement, Poe, Gail Hatcher's raven, perches on a drying stand covered in damp gothic attire, reading a copy of *The Importance of Being Earnest*. It watches the teenage girl peel a bloody gauze pad from her neck, revealing a small, but still weeping, bite wound.

"You really should get that looked at," Poe tells Gail in a cracked, but cultured voice. "There's no telling where those... people have been."

Gail looks over her shoulder at the bird as it turns the pages with prehensile wingtips and she knows it's right.

"We're providing a service," Director Jason Numan tells me from behind his large desk in the office of AnthroPets. "From ancient history and folklore across the globe, through Beatrix Potter and Disney and onto modern day Anime, the anthropomorphisation of animals has been widespread in human cultures. We're just making use of modern advances in genetics to give people what they want."

Director Numan catches sight of something on his computer screen and is momentarily distracted, before he continues. "True, the technology has been widely adopted and advanced by the military, but so was barbed wire and tinned food. And the idea of animals used in battle... well, one needs only look at the history of humanity.

"We at AnthroPets are making use of this new technology to give people pets they can really and truly treat like human beings. So far, and with the aforementioned assistance of the military, we've perfected the process with all forms of canine, feline and avian species. We're pushing the boundaries of this new technology towards equine and are already having significant progress with many breeds of fish and some favourite family rodents.

"Primarily we raise the subject animal's IQ, provide the ability for speech, modify bone structure to allow for bipedal movement and either adapt, or in the case of avian breeds, create prehensile appendages. Mostly, we just give out opposable thumbs."

Director Numan frowns, reading more from the screen, before returning his attention to me. "Yes, there have been tragedies and accidents along the way, but think of it like this; if a mistreated Border Collie has the emotional range to comprehend and the manual dexterity to pull the trigger of a shotgun, then isn't that better than said animal suffering such abuse?"

# I Stood and Watched

Danny O'Connor

I stood and watched as no. 1 sprang from your loins. Fist and
head first. A superman unbound. Still
connected by the umbilical cord

I stood and watched as no. 3 was presented behind the glass
screen. All happed up in a tight blanket
held with tenderness by a bearded hulk
of an Australian doctor. Whisked away
lobster-red with too many corpuscles

I stood and watched as no. 2 lay naked except for his birth-
blood. Fighting with each breath for life

I stood and watched as you gyrated round and round on the
dance floor of the Students' Union

I stood and watched as you swithered over the choosing of your
diamond engagement ring

I didn't stand and watch as we coupled and made love with each
other that 1$^{st}$ night

I stood and watched in my mind's eye, as I got up from our
marriage bed and bayed at the moon

# Triple Threat Treat

Samuel McCann

It was dark, cold and wet. Jonathon knew he shouldn't be here – Central Park at midnight – but where else was a seventeen-year-old runaway to go, when he had virtually nothing but the clothes on his back and the contents of a hastily-packed duffle bag to get by with?

'I just need some place dry,' he thought to himself, exhausted and almost pleading for respite with the world around him. 'Somewhere to sit and think for a minute.'

"What's that?" he said out loud as he noticed flickering light through the bushes some way off.

The prospect of some light or warmth invigorated him, and he found his legs carrying him towards it before he had even made the conscious decision to do so. Emerging from the foliage he found a stone arch occupied by a blazing oil drum and a ragged figure crouching within a shadowed recess. The figure did not stir at his approach, sitting as still as a gargoyle mounted on its perch.

"S-Sorry, man," Jonathon froze in the face of the hooded stranger. "I didn't know anyone was here. Do you mind if I...?"

"Not at all, kid," the stranger replied in a gravely voice, that was New Yorker through and through, as he tilted his head to reveal a crooked but warm smile. "Take a load off. I don't bite."

"Thanks, man," Jonathon breathed a sigh of relief before stepping into the glow, not taking his eyes off of the stranger.

"Not a problem," the wretch droned, raising a bottle, sheathed in brown paper, to his lips before then offering it to his guest. "Drink?"

"Sure, why not?" Jonathon replied after a moment's hesitation, keen to mask his desperation from his down-and-out host, as he plucked the bottle from the man's grasp before knocking it back.

"That'll put hairs on your chest, huh kid?" the down-and-out cackled and wheezed with laughter as Jonathon spluttered and composed himself.

"It's fine," Jonathon replied hoarsely, blanching just a little less on the second gulp, before handing it back. "Thanks."

"Don't mention it," the down-and-out replied, waving off Jonathon's thanks before drinking a healthy measure himself.

Silence ensued for a time whilst Jonathon acquainted himself with the heavenly warmth bestowed by the brazier, occasionally stealing a glance at his host. The man seemed harmless enough, Jonathon surmised, with his gaunt and heavily lined features indicating that he had lived a rough and unforgiving life on the streets for a great many years. If his face was anything to go by then he was nothing but skin and bone beneath the many layers of grime-encrusted clothing he wore.

"What's your story, kid?" the down-and-out asked him out of the blue.

"Huh?" Jonathon flinched.

"Everybody's got a story to tell," the man sneered, lifting his head to invite the light of the fire within the shadow of his hood and revealing a heavy brow and eyes so pale that he almost appeared blind. "Come on. What else we gonna do to pass the time, huh? Watch cable?"

"There's not much to tell," he replied nervously. "I'm Jonathon. I got sick of shit back home so I walked out and caught the first bus out of there. I just arrived this morning. So, here I am. And that's it – story of my life."

"Shame," the man sighed. "But I can sorta relate. My name's Marl, by the way."

"Nice to meet you," Jonathon replied without enthusiasm, his gaze lost in the fire as he contemplated the depth of his past.

Little else passed between them for some time, save for the occasional sharing of a draught of liquor, or as either of them shifted to alleviate their discomfort. All the while Jonathon continued gazing into the fire, until the dying glow threatened to vanish altogether. No sooner had the embers began to fade than Marl arose suddenly and made lots of indulgent noises as he stretched out all the crimps in his bones. Jonathon cringed at the ominous sounds of creaking and cracking that accompanied Marl's movements, wondering whether his bones could possibly still be intact.

"Time to call it a night," Marl remarked. "It'll be light soon and the cops'll be by any minute to move us on. For the benefit of the joggers and the tourists, of course. Nice knowing you, kid."

"What? Wait!" Jonathon started to his feet. "Where are you going?"

"Some place with a roof over it and no cops," Marl replied, already with his back to him as he began staggering into the brush.

"Can I come along?" the boy called out after him, abandoning any pretence of nonchalance, in light of his predicament.

"Sure, kid," Marl replied, concealing the satisfied sneer on his face as he continued walking. "Always room for one more. Follow me."

Jonathon set out warily after Marl as the man tottered off through the brush. Jonathon glanced over his shoulder occasionally as he went to make sure they weren't being followed. The last thing he needed right now was for the cops to show up and put him in the slammer for vagrancy or – worse yet – send him back home to his bastard stepfather. Some risks were worth taking, he thought, looking on as Marl continued to lead them through the foliage.

Marl meanwhile meandered drunkenly though the woods, singing garbled snatches from old songs in between falling to the ground every now and then. Jonathon was mortified as Marl proceeded to relieve himself against a tree, and averted his eyes to continue watching the path they had tread in favor of observing him pee. It was then that he heard sounds of a commotion heading their way, suddenly spying five silhouettes moving through the gray light of dawn towards them. He could tell by their movements and behavior that they were high or something, and suspected it would be wise not to hang around long enough to find out if they were friendly or not.

"Marl, we gotta get out of here, now," he whispered urgently, hurriedly pushing the other man along.

"Ah, what's the rush?" the man chuckled, having barely finished his business. "It'll just be some gang or other coming to beat the bejesus out of us, is all."

"Are you serious?" Jonathon almost shrieked, pushing the man along more forcefully. "Then let's get going, man!"

Marl eventually led them to a stone pipeline that jutted out of a steep incline overlooking a narrow streambed. The metal grille, which had once barred the entrance, had eroded, and all that was left were jagged, rusty teeth around its circumference.

"In here," Marl said, half-heartedly indicating the narrow tunnel, before falling face down into the dirt and muttering drunken curses.

"Marl! Come on," Jonathon fretted, his anxious eyes scanning the brush as jubilant cries and threats arose from their pursuers close by.

Hoisting the man to his feet, Jonathon draped one of Marl's arms over his shoulder before stooping with him to enter the tunnel and plunging them into darkness. Light from overhead grilles further ahead lit the way as he struggled breathlessly along with Marl's dead weight imposing on him. They emerged into a high-ceilinged chamber with many grilles and spillways leading into it, as well as metal platforms leading to higher levels. Not waiting for Marl's instructions, he carried the man up the nearest set of stairs to a relatively dry side tunnel, littered with enough evidence to suggest that someone lived there. No sooner had he set Marl down on a pile of soiled blankets than a low growl arose from the shadows.

Jonathan stepped back startled as a pair of glowing eyes and the wide, slavering maw of some hellish beast emerged from the darkness, forcing him to abandon Marl as he turned and fled back the way he had come... straight into the arms of their pursuers.

"Guys! There's no time for this now!" Jonathon protested, flailing wildly as he was passed from pillar to post among them whilst they jeered and cajoled him. "There's a monster..."

His pleas froze in the air as he came to the realization that his tormentors were not normal looking; their eyes were feral and filled with malice, their brows twisted and cruel, and their wide, sneering mouths bearing predatory fangs that revealed their savage natures. Aside from their terrifying visages they were also incredibly strong and he felt utterly helpless in their grasp. All he could do now was pray for a miracle.

He almost wept with relief as a great, hulking monstrosity like a hairless, red ape with horns sprouting from its head, burst in on the scene, scattering Jonathon and his tormentors and dashing him to the ground, before chaos ensued within the shadowed chamber.

"Marl? Marl!" the gang leader's voice rang out as the crimson monstrosity cornered him against the near wall. "Call your beast off, God damn it! What gives here?"

"Marl? What the...?" Jonathon spat, rising unsteadily to his feet as Marl sauntered into the light with his hood down to reveal his craggy and hairless features.

"That's enough, Rav," Marl asserted with newfound confidence and presence in his voice. "Sorry, Park. He gets so carried away when he's hungry. And Ravener Demons have no love of vampires at the best of times, as you know."

"Marl? I... I don't understand," Jonathon sobbed as he looked with horrified realization upon the down-and-out, whose bearing had changed dramatically since their first meeting. "You're one of them?"

"Nah, I'm something else, kid," Marl replied with a mote of regret in his voice. "We all gotta eat, and us Marrow Demons can only sustain ourselves with one thing..."

"The marrow from your bones, sweetmeat," sneered the lead vampire, stepping forth, flanked by his leering, un-human entourage, as they headed off any hope of escape. "Of course, first of all, we'll drain every drop of your blood. Then Rav will strip all the flesh off your bones, and Marl - our resident parasite here - will polish off the rest. Whatever's left of you will just float off down the sewers, as though you had never been. Any objections?"

Thinking fast, Jonathon replied in desperation, "You can't eat me! I have AIDS! That's why I ran away from home. I'm gay and... and my father, he didn't understand so..."

"Save it, kid," said Park. "You might be queer, but you got virgin written all over you. Besides, disease don't scare us. Does it matter to you, Marl? What about Rav here?"

Marl shook his head resolutely to both questions whilst the Ravener Demon only growled in response.

"So, looks like we got ourselves a takeout, three-course meal here, boys. Whaddya say?" the vampire sneered, rubbing his hands together whilst regarding the boy as though he were the proverbial turkey at Thanksgiving.

"Just get it over with!" Marl barked, before adding more softly. "Sorry, kid. It'll be quick. And believe me, you're better off this way anyhow. A life on the streets is no place for a boy your age."

With that, Marl turned his back and melted into the shadows, abandoning the boy to his fate.

"Kiss my ass, Marl!" Jonathon retorted after him, standing tall and baring his pulsing wrists to his captors. "I hope you choke, you bastards."

Marl crouched in the darkest recess of the tunnels, far from the scene of the slaughter with his hands clasped tightly over his ears in an attempt to drown out Jonathon's cries. Though the cries were not lasting, Marl continued to hear them long after they had ceased. In the ensuing solitude when he emerged to feast upon the boy's bones, it was with tears rolling down his craggy cheeks all the while.

'Some days, being a monster sucks,' he thought.

# Terror Thought

Danny O'Connor

The terror thought clubbed in at me again today. Just the same as it did yesterday.

All the clichés still work. My blood ran cold. I was numbed. I couldn't think straight. It's just too hard to come up with innovative ways to describe the gut-wrenching terror – there, I'm clicheing again. But it is.

The panic the terror thought creates inside me is unedifying. I've never had the presence of mind to even move, never mind go to the mirror. But now, in my more relaxed position, my mind's eye sees me, when the terror thought clubs me, as all pale and wan with my features contorted in fear. I don't know how many heartbeats it takes for the terror to subside because when I'm held in its thrall I can't think. No straight or even crooked thoughts come to mind. It's like there's a power outage in those little electrical synapses that pass messages along my cerebral cortex.

'Coping mechanism'. Now there's a phrase that conjures up absolutely zilch in my brain. I've been taught that I'm supposed to do the things that I've been trained to do to roll myself back from the precipice that the terror thought has frog-marched me to. The problem is that when my blood has froze and the shilling has run out in the meter in my head I can't remember a fucking thing – never mind some pious little mantra designed to scare away the big bad wolf of terror.

When the terror thought hits, the concept of it is too awesome for me to hold in such a pitiful container as my brain. If I was smarter, or more learned, or both, even then I know that I still couldn't handle the enormity of it. So when it comes it devastates me until it deflates of its own accord just enough for me to be able to push it outside of me and bolt the fabled stable door until the next time.

# Words

Craig Murray

Be a thorn in someone else's side
I have enough pain in my life
Words that cut me like a knife
You know this isn't helpful
I could drag myself down to your level
And bring your world crashing to the ground
With little effort
I could say things just as hurtful
Trust me, you wouldn't want me to be around
I could become just like you
But I don't want to
I don't care about settling the score
I have no interest in fighting with you anymore.

# Miss Narcissus

J. B. Quinn

Dancing butterfly dead eyes
Flitting from victim to victim
Sickly-sweet, white chocolate smile
Satin-bowed, rose-scented bile
Cruel-laden comments, politely delivered
Two-faced permanent façade
Storyteller of hyped-up-tripe
Bullshit pedalled, like riding a bike

Slander slips from your platinum tongue
Harm wherever your gaze falls
Unblemished lies; pockmarked truth
Honeyed incongruence drips from your mouth
Feigned empathy of a shallow spirit
Empty heart of a guiltless mind
Sincerely polished act of sophistry
Too sweet to be wholesome, thin veneer
Gathering the naïve like wild flowers
Offering pure open-ended loyalty
Sycophantly, sucking up to deemed superiors
Exploiting, then dismissing judged inferiors

Paint-stripping harshness of the kind
Reminiscent of a narcissistic or sociopathic mind
Relentless march of perfect selfishness and greed
Like the creeping vine or the strangling weed
Miss Narcissus, this ode is to you
To thine self, you cannot even be true
I could pity your insecure need to be powerfully rich
If you weren't such a top class, award winning bitch

Still, it may be a little unfair to single you out
When there are many more like you, lurking about
Why, when those of your type; who are a minority
Should you be found wielding power over the majority?
When equality is suffocated by might over right
When good men and women turn away from the fight
When convention tramples the weak in favour of the strong
Silent consensus consolidates your control, and helps it along.
As you prey on the herd, it stampedes and falls
The justice of hell; exacting no retribution at all
As your misdeeds go unpunished, humanity's last hope
Is that you dog-eat-dogs, devour one another and choke.

# I Don't Feel Poetic

Danny O'Connor

I don't feel poetic today
The muse has gone away
My mind has gone astray
Yes, I feel apathetic today
And I know what you'll say
And you'll want it to hold sway
"Don't fall into your usual traps
Pull yourself up by the bootstraps
No ifs, buts, or perhaps
Just give yourself a good shake
and for God's sake - stay awake
If you can't be real: be a fake
Don't dare give in
You know it's a sin
So just make a din
Make like you're alive
At least from nine to five
That's when you have to strive
Like a bee in a hive
Extend life and limb
In life's give and take
Don't dare relapse
Into your sonorous way"

# Bewilderment

William N. Dyer

Jennifer woke to silence. She was not yet aware of what had happened. She looked at the clock radio. It displayed nine am. She was late by her standards. Why had the radio not woken her? She would have no time for her breakfast. "Why the hell not? After all I'm on flexi," she thought.

She always had breakfast before she did her toilette. The needs of the inner body took precedence over the outer.

She got out of bed and did her morning inspection in the full-length mirrored wardrobe. There she stood a slightly beefed-up five foot six authentic blonde. She was still looking good even for a single, thirty-something.

Into the kitchen and on with the electric kettle. Two slices of wholegrain bread into the toaster. Next, to the front door, to pick-up the newspaper. She liked to start her mornings in peace: coffee, toast and marmalade, and a read of the paper. And today was proving to be very congenial.

She was sitting at the breakfast bar reading the paper when she looked up. She saw the toast had popped up and steam was streaming from the kettle spout. What had distracted her in the paper? Nothing. "She was fazed from getting up late," she thought.

She had bought this flat for several reasons. First, it was in the West End, the cultural centre of Glasgow. Second, it was modern but spacious. No work needing done and plenty of room. Jennifer did a lot of living-in. She enjoyed reading and listening to music and was very secure with her own company. She would at least be able to enjoy those pleasures most of the time.

To the bathroom to wash. On with the shower. It was one of those large walk-in types with no door, cool, and a great feature. It's all quiet today and that usually happened after she got water in her ears. She was becoming uneasy. Something more than being late was amiss.

She got dressed in her neat two-piece business trouser-suit. A quick check in the mirror and she'd be ready to go. To the phone to order a taxi to take her into the city centre. She'd phone the office to let them know she was coming in later. There was nothing scheduled for this morning.

She lifted the phone, but there was no dial tone. That was typical for telecoms, not working when you need them, a bit like the police, buses and so many alleged modern amenities. She took her mobile out of her satchel and although it was on and had apparently dialled the taxicab company's number, there was no sound. There was no sound.

It hit her. There was no sound. She had not heard a thing since she had woken this morning. Utter silence. Nothing above the threshold of hearing. Her flat was usually quiet. She'd been late up avoiding the noise associated with the normal rush hour. What had seemed so pleasant now was intimidating.

# Valedictory

Eddie McGonnell

The hills were alive with sunlight cascading down like golden streams of promise. The dawn chorus launched into its repertoire of melodic noise and the night receded shamefacedly, almost as if its threat of darkness had felt intimidated in the face of nature's orchestral symphony.

The lone gamekeeper treading the narrow path turned up his collar to protect himself against the first smirr of rain. It would be another day of walking the land, observing, noting, reporting on the day-to-day running of the huge estate. He loved when he had these precious, magic moments to himself. That wonderful sense of isolation when he felt as if he were the only person on the planet, experiencing the gold of the day and a quietness that was profound and powerful. He always felt comfortable in a world inhabited by one person, especially when he was so close to nature. He had never married in life, somehow the attractions of domestic harmony had failed to impress him and he was now left with nature as his quiet, unassuming bride. But Eden never had any permanence and there were always the mundane matters of life to be attended to. There were, for instance, the grouse-shooters.

They came here, he thought, and strutted around like little gods with their tweed jackets and their ridiculously pretentious manner of conversing with one another. He hated the patronising way that they addressed the gamekeepers. And the beaters, of course, were treated like coolie labour during the last days of Empire.

The grouse-shooters wined, dined, shot and played out their petty little dramas amidst the rural splendour of the Scottish Highlands. It was almost as if a tiny corner of Edwardiana had been preserved to allow these silly people to indulge in their juvenile pursuits.

He came round the bend and froze at what he saw before him. A young deer lay on the ground covered in blood. It was obvious that it had been butchered for its venison as other parts lay strewn across the path. He knelt down and touched it: it was still slightly warm.

He fought to control the anger which welled up inside him. It was a young deer with its life in front of it. Not unlike some young, adolescent boy looking forward to manhood, but men had raised their ugly hands to ensure that his life was cut short at their behest. He had been engaged in deer culls before when it became necessary to control the number of deer running wild. But this was different, it was a barbaric act committed with a total disregard of nature.

Whoever had committed the deed had left in great haste; it would not prove too difficult to follow their trail through the woods.

He set off in pursuit immediately, a gentle man who was not easily aroused to feelings of violence, but when it came to the killing of defenceless animals especially in such gruesome circumstances, the unbridled loathing coursed through his veins like a poison.

He crouched stealthily as he walked, making himself a difficult target. You could never tell with these people, if cornered, they were just as liable to take human life as that of a young deer.

He remembered once as a young boy his father had taken him to see the film, The Last of the Mohicans. The Native Indians in the film had managed to track their quarry by their awareness of a broken leaf; a scuffed footprint; or a loose pebble on the trail. He had watched fascinated at the woodsman-ship of the Iroquois and Huron and ever since had immersed himself in the art of tracking.

He had been walking through the woods his gun at the ready for some considerable time and was beginning to feel that he had lost his quarry, when just after fording a small stream he came across the killer.

The man's back was turned towards him. It appeared to the gamekeeper as if the slaughterer was further butchering the young deer on the banks of the stream. A twig snapped under the gamekeeper's foot and the man twisted round as if a regiment of soldiers had arrived.

They looked at each other across the brief distance which separated them. The face looking at him showed no signs of surprise, on the contrary, the unshaven features presented a face of quiet cruelty. He was standing with a bloodstained knife in his right hand and the front of his shirt was smeared bright red.

It was the killer's eyes, however, that frightened him more than anything. They had an expression of controlled malice. It was as if the gamekeeper had invaded the killer's own private ritual. In another place, on another day, far removed from here, perhaps that same cold, barbaric *Homo sapiens* would have been a player in an orgy of bloodletting.

The man had not uttered a word but kept staring at him with those ice-cold blue eyes. He then, with great deliberation, wiped the blood-stained knife on the leg of his trousers. The chilling thought occurred to the gamekeeper that the movement presaged some sacrificial act.

They looked at each other for another split second and again the gamekeeper felt as if he were facing something primeval; something which could not respond to any civilised code. He could see that the man was younger than he and was of a burly stature. If it came to a fight the gamekeeper would be overwhelmed, of that he was sure. Even if he did manage to apprehend him, the most the criminal could expect from the courts would be a fine and probably probation for a period of time. How about the young deer, he thought? Gunned down in its innocence, never to know the exhilaration of running free with the herd, or drinking from some cool highland stream.

All of a sudden he was tired of being the nice guy. Of always doing the right thing even when he felt that his character was being submerged beneath a polite and well-mannered smile. It was a painful truth, but sometimes society expected too much. He lifted his rifle to his shoulder and took aim. For once in his life he was going to do what he wanted to do.

It was payback time.

The hunter awoke with the feeling of total depression. Another dawn meant another laborious ritual of small, repetitive demands. At times he felt as if he were drowning in a sea of mind-sapping domestic routine. The struggle to ensure that his family survived amidst the minefields of the complexities of modern living was at times mind numbing. It wasn't easy being unemployed with a wife and five children to feed.

He felt that his life had been one of unremitting failure, a merry-go round of bleak existence where there had been very few shafts of sunlight. People kept reminding him of the nice wife and family that he had and there was no doubt that his wife and children were a great source of pride and pleasure to him, but there is an inner recess in every man's mind, that little niche of quiet contemplation, that craves some kind of personal recognition and he felt that, so far, he was a nobody.

His happiest days had been spent with his father. He was an only child and his parents had doted on him. His father was known in their village as Big Alex and had been renowned for his hunting skills.

Big Alex would take his young son into the blue hills which surrounded their village and with impeccable poaching skills would ensure that their cooking pot was never empty. The young boy adored his father and the local hunting trips allowed him to imagine that he was a mighty hunter capturing all sorts of wild beasts. No one ever bothered about the morality of poaching - the idea that they were stealing. Morality was for bible thumping zealots, Big Alex would claim, and hadn't God created this earth to be enjoyed?

It all started to go wrong for him when he was six years old. He could still remember that terrible day running home after school and sensing something was wrong with the amount of strangers that were in the house.

The dreadful news was that his mother and father had been killed on a level crossing, in their little second-hand car.

People kept hugging him and crying over him and saying the totally inadequate things that people say at a time like that, but no one could possibly know how a young boy of that age felt at such a calamitous time in his life.

He had no close relatives who were prepared to look after him so he suffered the ultimate childhood horror of being put into care. He couldn't honestly say that the people were cruel to him. He was fed and clothed and educated to the accepted social standards of the time. It was just that there was a throbbing, emotional pain inside of him, which no matter how long he was there, never went away.

He was never an academic high-flyer at school and normally sat at the back of the class attempting to be as unobtrusive as possible. He was dyslexic and wasn't properly diagnosed, so his world of learning became one of struggling within the confines of word-blindness. A cry for help that had gone unheeded.

He had left school with the most basic of certificates and had wandered from one dead-end job into another. He didn't meet, fall in love and get married; he got married because he could no longer bear the purgatory of loneliness. His marriage to a local girl gave him a degree of stability, but as the babies came along he found that he was living a little more desperately each day.

He derived a great deal of pleasure from taking his only son out poaching with him. The boy thoroughly enjoyed the experience and he felt that there *was* a rapport building up between them, one which almost equalled the bond that had been formed between he and his father.

He had called the boy Alex, after his father and it seemed like the boy was adept for this contest with nature. The boy had an instinctive flair for poaching. He hunted with a keen eye and he would always be successful, even on the most discouraging of days.

He was not hunting today, however.

He turned to poaching to supplement his meagre income so at least the family didn't starve. Through the years he acquired a high degree of woodsman-ship on a par, perhaps, with his beloved father, until this day when he found himself looking across the barrel of a gun.

It was amazing what you noticed in a situation like that. The first thing he noticed was the gamekeeper's military style moustache. It was an intimidating appendage made famous by successive generations of British Army officers. He wondered if it frightened the deer.

The gamekeeper had raised his rifle and his intention was crystal clear: but it was vigilantism no matter how one looked at it. What gave this man the right to take human life? He had killed a deer. So what! Would the gamekeeper have shot a royal prince for committing a similar act? The difference was the prince wouldn't have had five children to feed, just the admiration of the chattering classes.

He looked the gamekeeper in the eye: the rifle, unwavering, was pointing straight at him. If the gamekeeper pressed the trigger then his life would come to an end, beside some gurgling, highland stream that would soon run red.

The voices were screaming inside his head in stark contrast to the almost unearthly stillness of the scene. He started to find breathing difficult and found himself sweating profusely. It wasn't enough that the gamekeeper wanted to kill him, that was never enough for these military types. He wanted to humiliate him, to have him beg for mercy. Well, that wasn't going to happen.

The sun was now declining; gloaming time. That almost surreal part of the day when the purple colours of nature enveloped everything in their ghostly light and when, Big Alex maintained, elves danced amongst the trees.

He wanted to shout at the man that he was Big Alex's son, the true inheritor; the keeper of the keys; Oberon. As if this would have earned him some kind of passport to life or a last minute reprieve from Caesar and the screaming hordes.

He saw the gamekeeper's finger tighten on the trigger.

## Epilogue

You go up the steep hillside that is covered in bracken and gorse with, here and there, a sprinkling of small purple flowers that lends the hillside a quiet, splash of colour. It comes as a surprise when you stumble on the clearing, it is almost as if it has no right to be there. It is obvious that human hands have pushed back the wilderness as there are two well- tended graves in the centre of the clearing.

The first grave is like so many other graves with a poignant recording of a husband and wife who have passed on a number of years before. The other grave, however, is striking in its appearance.

The gilt letters set against black marble convey a family's sorrow, but it is the illustration at the side of the lettering that is arresting. A figure with a bow and arrow, Nimrod the mighty hunter, stands majestically on the headstone, below the illustrated figure is written one word - *Alex*.

# Justice

Craig Murray

You always thought you were one step ahead
So cocky you never cared what you said
Be aware someday your words will come back to haunt you
My river of hate runs deep and is close to overflowing
Every time I see your face the feeling keeps on growing
I'm not spending my time crossing my fingers
Wishing you would die
But if I heard it happened it wouldn't make me cry
You will get what you deserve
For trying to drag my name though the dirt
Justice will be served
But not by me
If there's a Heaven you'll be turned away
If there's a Hell
Your reservation's been made
And the Devil is waiting outside your door with your key.

# Claustrophobia

Claire Szemis

He didn't like the idea of sleeping inside a coffin.

It didn't seem natural; you were only supposed to lie in coffins once you were dead, lifeless, gone, already decomposing. So it was quite understandable that every inch of Alexander's body was fighting against the very idea. He wasn't dead yet, so why should he lie in something so uncomfortable and stiff? He'd only be asleep in the bloody thing but the wrongness of it terrified him. Coffins were for the dead, and the undead, and he was still alive and mortal with absolutely no intention of dying in the not so distant future. He was however shortly going to join the undead and that meant sleeping in a dark, cold and enclosed box.

Alexander already felt claustrophobic.

He'd come over all funny when he overheard his father asking Dmitri what size would be most appropriate and he had nearly fallen off the chair when his uncle suggested one just like his own. He and Dmitri may have been similar in build so the estimate was correct, but it was extraordinary to look into the man's room and see it lying there and to know that his own would be similar. Alex had found himself unable to deal with the whole horrible eventuality of it and he refused to go anywhere near his uncle's room for several hours.

He was still unable to face the long wooden box long after his father and uncle departed for the night but if there was something Alex hated more than a life in a box, it was his own cowardice. So it was with stubbornness worthy of any Vasile that Alexander snuck back up the stairs to investigate his future place of rest. He bypassed Dmitri's bedroom and went into his father's instead because at least that would be a little roomier, and a little more comforting.

Alexander waited until there was no one on the landing before he slipped into his parents' room and shut the door behind him, his eyes automatically falling upon that horrible thing which ran along one wall. He sighed to himself, steadying his trembling hands before he approached the coffin, avoiding all the floorboards that tended to creak so no one would know what he was up to. He stood before it for several moments, trying to reconcile the idea that he wouldn't actually be dead in a box.

He placed his hand upon the lid and blew out a breath, mustering all the determination he could to swing open the lid and peer within. It wasn't entirely what he expected. He was sure the inside would look pretty much the same as the outside, all wood and plain and miserable. Alex was surprised to find that the whole interior was padded so it could cushion the body from all angles. He pressed down on it but it still didn't seem too comfortable. It actually seemed a little morbid; why did the dead need cushioning anyway?

Alex paused for a moment, twitching his head to the side and listening to make sure there was no one around, before he stood up on the step and very awkwardly clambered inside. He stretched out his legs before him, frowning when he saw exactly how big his father was compared to himself, but he didn't lie down right away. It was enough for Alex to just sit for a moment, sit and get used to the slightly enclosed sensation.

He lay back slowly, his hands sliding down the sides of the coffin before he was completely horizontal. Lying there, so rigidly and with little room to manoeuvre, he began to fidget. Alexander didn't like lying on his back, it created irritating pressure points on certain parts of his spine. He preferred lying on his front with his arm under his pillow, and there was no way in hell was he going to be able to sleep in this position.

But he still hadn't completed the whole experience and it was with a rapid acceleration of his heartbeat that he reached up and wrapped his fingers around the corner of the lid, pulling it slowly before jerking his hand away and allowing it to clatter down above him. Everything went pitch black, there was no way a single shred of light could penetrate the enclosed space. He couldn't see a damn thing; he couldn't even see the sides of the coffin but for some reason that made him feel worse. Instead of the walls boxing him in, it was the darkness that oppressed him, sitting heavily upon his chest and crushing him.

He closed his eyes and counted down from one hundred so he had something else to think about. But halfway through he started to think about other things, like the glimpse of Vikki's bra-strap when he had walked home with Sully and his girlfriend. He thought about his guitar and mentally practised his chords, humming a little bit of

Blink 182 under his breath. It wasn't so bad lying in a coffin with your eyes closed because you could have been anywhere. It was only when you opened them back up again and saw the black nothingness around you that it became damn scary.

Alex smiled to himself, relieved that he had at least given the coffin a chance. He didn't like it at all but he had still conquered his fear and that gave his rather fragile self esteem the boost it so desperately needed. Congratulating himself on his fortitude, he reached up and pushed against the coffin lid, expecting it to swing back and fall away to the side.

But it didn't.

It remained very resolutely closed and no matter how much he pushed the lid would not budge, almost as if it had gotten stuck when he allowed it to slam down. Trapped within, he had no idea that his father's coffin required a lot of upper body strength which the teenager didn't have and without someone to help him there was no way he could free himself.

Alexander felt himself beginning to panic as he pressed and pushed and thumped upon the coffin lid, trying desperately to knock it open. His heart raced as he struggled, his hands sliding down uselessly on the wood as he tried to make his escape.

"*This is a pretty fine mess you've gotten yourself into this time,*" his inner critic mocked him, sounding rather disconcertingly like his horrible grandfather, "*It looks like you are going to end up dead in a box, not just undead in a box. How could you be so stupid?*"

He groaned loudly, frustrated that life always seemed to be making a fool of him. He could see the headlines already- TEENAGER FOUND DEAD IN COFFIN. It would be a rather good thing in some ways, it wasn't exactly something you could live down; dying of asphyxiation simply because you really were that stupid.

Alex wondered exactly how long he would last inside his father's coffin. He wanted to bash and scream upon the lid like a madman until someone heard his screams and came running but surely that would use up all his oxygen? He would die faster if he made such a ruckus and he began to evaluate how long he could hold out, whether he would live until his father came home if he lay still and only breathed in tiny little gasps, or whether he should take a gamble, scream like hell and use up all his oxygen in the chance someone could free him immediately.

Either way he was going to end up embarrassed. He began to wish that he had used Dmitri's coffin after all because, while his uncle would mercilessly tease him and crack thousands of jokes over his plight, at least he wouldn't make Alex explain himself. His parents would force him to stand and tell them exactly why he decided to trap himself in his father's coffin and Alexander hated being held up to such scrutiny. He could only hope and pray that his younger brother, Nicholas, would hear him instead because at least he could tell him to keep his big mouth shut.

Alex took a deep breath and slammed his palm against the lid, trying to create the most amount of noise with the least amount of effort. He didn't shout out, he didn't scream, oxygen was too damn precious for that. He just slammed the palm of his hand repeatedly, and hoped that the sound would alert someone to his rather unfortunate presence. Eventually it did, and he tensed all over when he heard his parent's door creak open.

Then there was silence. Alex waited, too focused on trying to hear who his saviour was to think about breathing. He strained to listen, his stomach tying itself in knots as he heard the slow, dragging footsteps. Someone was approaching him, but only at a leisurely pace because saving him wasn't that much of a priority. The footfalls stopped just outside the coffin and silence reigned once more. There was something in the silence that made all the hairs on his body stand on end; something alive, cruel and hateful.

He twitched when he heard the pitter patter of someone drumming their fingers on the lid, and Alex felt like he had been drenched in ice water when he heard a voice say, "My, my. This is a pretty fine mess you've gotten yourself into this time."

"Shit," Alex cursed. If anyone could have saved him, why the hell did it have to be his grandfather? Death was preferable to being saved by that hateful, horrible old man. Fate had not been kind to Jan Vasile and nothing in his life had turned out how he had planned or how he had wanted. All the years of denial had turned him bitter and he was never more sour than when he dealt with his unfortunate grandson.

Jan chuckled, and still he didn't move to open up the lid. "I'm sure you had a reason," the old man laughed, "a stupid one, but you will have had one nonetheless. You must be feeling pretty embarrassed in there, poor little thing trapped in dear old daddy's coffin?"

"Lid's stuck," Alex said dumbly, hating Jan and hating himself for being so intimidated by the old man.

"How awful," Jan said with a mock tragic air, teasing him, "you must be so scared, running out of oxygen maybe. I should let you out, shouldn't I? It's what the older, more mature people do, run around bailing the little less sensible ones out of trouble. But I'm getting old and tired, I may not have the strength."

"You won't help me?" the teenager fretted.

"You have to ask me," his grandfather replied.

"Help me out, Grandad?"

"I didn't hear the word please," the embittered old vampire chuckled, waiting for the teenager to speak again. "I won't help you if I don't hear please."

Alex took a deep breath, trying to control the fury in his chest and all the embarrassment that enveloped his anger. He seethed through his teeth, "Please help me? Please?"

"Of course I will help you then," Jan said, "it's just that I really don't have the strength to lift such a big lid. I'll have to fetch your father, won't I?"

"But he's gone," Alex told him. It was bad enough dealing with Jan's cruelty; he wasn't looking forward to his father's disappointment as well.

"Oh no," his grandfather replied, "he came back. The silly fool left that ridiculous mobile phone contraption behind. Shall I go and shout on him? You really need saving, otherwise he'll come home tomorrow morning and find you dead. I'm sure it would break his heart."

Alexander's eyes stung with shame, his whole body shaking, mortified. He couldn't understand why Jan enjoyed tormenting him. And why was he always his grandfather's target? What made him so special to make Jan bully him so wholeheartedly?

But he couldn't voice any of those questions, and his heart sank as he heard the contemptible old man turn away and walk back out of the room, leaving him alone within the seemingly decreasing space. The darkness sat hard upon his chest and he feared he would lose all the air to breathe far quicker than he had previously imagined. He could only lie there, staring up into nothingness, hating Jan and despising himself.

But trapped within this nothingness he did decide one thing. He did not want a coffin, even if he was undead. He wouldn't have one and his father would just have to make other arrangements. That was, of course, if Jan really had left to retrieve his father. Otherwise he was going to spend the rest of his life in this box and life in a box really was better than no life at all, no matter how short it could turn out to be.

He lay there thinking about it, silently thankful, "Well, at least I'm not dead. Yet."

# The Vampires of Armour Street

Alexander J. Cunningham

The East End tenement on Armour Street is derelict. Forgotten in the city. The walls, cracked and crumbling, are graffiti-scrawled and every window is covered with a sheet of steel. A larger sheet covers the back door, with the front door's plate of rusted metal hinged, but padlocked.

There are other tenements on Armour Street and around the nearby area, all suffering from the same neglect, or worse. A few are nothing but fire-blackened shells, while others still hold the flickering light of a TV; a clue to its occupancy. And on the street, the handful of cars speak of the same abandonment and decay, with more than one playing victim to an insurance claim of necessity.

It's close to evening, with the sun setting in the smoke-filled sky, when the man arrives. His name is Peter Summers and he's dressed in heavy work clothes and carries two large picnic coolers in his gloved hands. He pauses at the plate steel door, unlocking each padlock and placing them into his pocket, before opening the door and stepping inside. He pulls the steel door closed.

"Dracula had good PR," Peter tells me over a coffee in a nearby café. His strong, weathered fingers trace scars on the formica table and there's an expression of dismay on his fifty-something face. "Dracula was the first, but from then to now and the string of new high school nonsense, there's always been a directive to make them look cool and dangerous, sexy and smart. But above all cool." He shakes his head. "Even Noseferatu, the closest in physical terms, is still overblown. If only the truth were known."

A slice of cherry pie, red and dripping, is placed before Peter. He looks at it and smiles. "Take food, for instance." Peter cuts deep into the pie, the thick red sauce spilling from the cracked wound on the crust. "The blood pours through the body, watering and nourishing the flesh, but without the work of major organs like the liver and kidneys to treat it, the blood becomes something akin to poison within thirty-six hours. Sometimes less. The heart works overtime trying to push the tarry sludge through atrophied or collapsing veins, but it's a losing battle."

"I tried to take Warfarin to water down what I was feeding on," Harv says. He's seventeen and has been that age for close to eleven years. His body is hairless and slender, with skin so thin and pale that his veins can be seen. They trace around his slight frame in bright crimson shades, like a patient with an infection and fever. "I was trying to make it last longer in my body. To flow better, but it always ends the same." Harv grimaces, showing receding gums that make his teeth look like a mouthful of gravestones. "It always ends with the hunger."

"I've tried them on various blood based products," Peter says, cutting into the wedge of pie. "Synthetic and animal were worse than useless. Real animal blood is tolerable, but it wouldn't be much more than bread and water to me.

"I need to seek out human donors. That's where cash for blood makes those less fortunate a little better off and my wards a little better fed. I'd tried to make contacts within the city hospitals, but they were greedy. Not to mention the fact that the blood stored there was intended for the living to survive. Not the dead to exist."

"I used to feed from a willing few in the Lost Souls night club here in the city," Katie admits. She runs her thin, crooked hands over her smooth, bald head and blinks away something. A tear rolls from her albino red eyes. Eyes that have seen the fall of empires. "There's nothing like the taste of the real thing. And from a real vein." She shudders, the pleasure still clear in her mind. "It's like nothing you can imagine."

Katie shakes her head, dismissing the memories. "But it's not safe. Not for them. The ones who offer themselves."

"I give these young, damaged kindred a sanctuary," Peter explains to me. "A place of safety, both from the world and from their own hunger. I use classic addiction methodology to wean them off the hunt and on to donated blood. From there, it's a matter of trying to acclimatise them. To make them children of the Politics of Forever, not victims of it."

"Victims?" Will asks, his face contorting into a sneer of contempt, his teeth white and primed. "Not me. I've left a trail of them across the years, but I was never one of them." He looks down at his taloned hands, surprised to find them not clenched into fists, but wringing themselves together. He breaks them away from each other, traitors to his heart and mind, and jams them into the pockets of his coat. "But it's the hunt that I miss. Selecting a target, tracking it to its lair, or a place where it's most vulnerable. Then the chase. Then the kill.

"But that was the old me," he corrects with forced control. "Before."

Peter smiles to the waitress who refills his coffee.

"There are countless numbers of origin myths for the vampire. They range from Cain, through Egyptian legend, Eastern mysticism, European folklore and modern day ideas of alien intervention and government conspiracies. All I can say is that they exist. They exist and have done for generations out of memory."

"Some of my kind talk about being at the Crucifixion," Katie says, her thin lips imitating a smile. "Woodstock, too. Or even in the bunker with Hitler." She looks at an old, folded piece of paper; a sepia photograph. "Those, or any one of a dozen other historical events.

"Most of this is nothing but posturing. To be honest, the simple act of living, and for so long, can be hard work." Katie folds the photograph, returning it to her pocket. "Just ask mortals."

"As well as providing a place for them to go where they can break the chain of bloodletting, I also offer a place where they can break away from the eternal struggle that exists between them. There are no politics, bloodfeuds, vampiric social conventions or anything else that makes one better than another. Simply put, this is a haven."

Peter sips his coffee, grimaces and adds sugar from a dispenser, before absently stirring. "So far I've seen close to eighty pass through my doors and on to a better life. Or not. I have twenty-six staying at the sanctuary at the moment, many are refuges from territorial warfare in a nearby district, with a handful looking to escape from a band of hunters.

"I'll provide this help for as long as I'm able, or until the funding dries up."

With the steel door shut, the tenement is in darkness. Peter places the two picnic iceboxes onto the floor and reaches into a pocket, producing a torch. He flicks it on and plays it across the floor, walls, and into the white faced, red-eyed figures ranged before him.

A mix of male and female, from mid-teens to late thirties. All hover, ready to reach, pounce and grab.

Peter opens one of the iceboxes, reaches through the crushed ice and pulls a bag of blood free. Their red, near glowing eyes watch it leave his hand and sail through the dark air.

And in a blur of movement, the vampires of Armour Street begin another night of feeding.

# A Boy's War

Eddie McGonnell

His poignant footsteps
Clatter down the rain-soaked streets
Seeking refuge
From the violent mob hunting him down.
His desperate legs are like pistons of pain,
Pumping fear through his body.
He will have to run the course
Of a one-sided war,
And hope that darkness can be his friend.
But batteries are running down,
And the heart- bursting effort of solo flight
Cannot be sustained.

Shouts and bottles are thrown
With all the malice of a Mills grenade,
And no-man's land stretches out to infinity.
Sodden street lamps paint a surreal pattern
Of flickering searchlights,
And the harbour of helping hands beckons
Like one last frenzied sanctuary
Of hope.

But the target is hit;
And red-coloured rainbows of life
Spread out in the rain,
Like pointing fingers of pain.
Shelters of silence will be erected
And behind drawn blinds
Whispers will be exchanged.
Fear is the currency
Of a self-preservation
That would rather not know about
Poignant footsteps.

# Second to You

Danny O'Connor

Second to You
Minute by minute,
I love you.
Hour by hour,
I am subject
To your object.

Day by day,
I see the way
I fail, You rail.
I am the snail,
To your comet.

No solace, no sonnet
Nothing that can last.
Can I tie fast.

To the sail of the craft,
That drives me half-daft,
Away with the tide,
With you upon it.

# The Sandy

Catherine Baird

I was scared to go into the water at the Sandy. It was a shallow part of the Luggie River and had a sandbank in the middle. I watched my brother jumping in but saw myself being swept away if I did it. He shouted at me to join in and screamed and laughed with everyone else as they ran to the water from across the muddy field.

It was a long walk to the Luggie and I was always scared the farmer would catch us going across his field. My brother told me that the fence we had to climb over was electrified, and that frightened me too. We always took a picnic: pieces on jam or cold meat, and orange juice diluted too much so that it resembled a urine sample and tasted bitter and dry. There was a rope swing at the Sandy, it hung over the deeper part of the river. I watched my brother swing out on it, landing with a yell and a splash. The water came up to his waist.

There was a hot summer when the Sandy almost dried up completely, it was only deep enough for paddling and one day I did go in, but with my plastic sandals on as I was afraid of fish biting me, or some other unnamed terror. A boy from our school died that day. He was kicking up water to soak all the kids who were paddling. There were no adults there and I only remember my mother going with us once. The boy was cautioned by a teenager whose little sister had complained and that was enough to stop him. He sat out on the bank then and dried his feet with his tee shirt. It was blue and had the Star Wars logo on it.

We saw someone opening their picnic and my big brother shared ours out between us. I was eating a hardboiled egg my mother had made when I saw the boy go past me and down to the water. He stepped in and went over to the far bank. The bank was steeper on that side and as he climbed up, he slipped. Two of the older boys were laughing at him and calling him a div. This was a new word for us. Someone had heard it on television and we were all experimenting with it. The boy gave them the fingers and laughed. He walked over to the tree with the swing and leaned out to try and catch the rope. It took him a few tries and when he got it the two older boys cheered.

He smiled and his face was red where the sun had burned him. He kicked away from the tree and swung back and forth to gather some force. When he let go he opened his arms wide as he fell towards the river and there was a splash. From where I was sitting I couldn't see him hitting the water but a boy near the edge shouted to him. The boy with the Star Wars tee shirt didn't get up. The teenage boys ran over and started shouting things and my brother ran to the water's edge as the teenagers slid down the bank and waded in. I stood up to see what was going on. The boys were standing knee deep in the water and pulling the Star Wars boy up. His head was lolling about and they dragged him up to the field by the arms.

My brother packed up our cups and threw away the crusts of his sandwich. He made me put the bottles and silver paper wrappers in his bag then grabbed my shoulder and told me to hurry up, that we had to go home. A crowd of other children ran with us across the field to get to the road. Some ran on ahead, my brother shouting for them to go to the farmhouse at the top of the hill to get help.

He took me home and my mother cuddled us for ages. She knocked the neighbour's doors and told them and one lady who lived in our street came in later to tell my mother that the boy had died. I was sitting halfway up the stairs as she said it. I could see the bottom of her legs through the living room doorway and I heard my mother say that it was terrible.

# Morning Stillness

J. B. Quinn

Sharp desperate screams
Cut through the window pane
Morning stillness shattered

High-pitched pleas
Claw and scratch the silent air
Drunken din of mindless disagreement

Passionately empty argument
Drifts on air of consciousness
Longing to be understood

Cruel intentions
Vindictively whispered on the wind
Ease the passage of idle gossip

One false word
Followed by another
Form to create the lie

Dull aching heavy head
Pulled from promised slumber
And soft warm pillow

Insight focused
Insomniac eyes held shut
Grudgingly blink open

Bleary bloodshot eyes
Stare into the mirror image
Manic-red glow of the alarm

Roar of testosterone
Sick thud of fist on flesh
Weary body slumps

Cold-blooded action
Hot-blooded reason
Death drains the last drop

Half cursing, half caring
Drawn into dreams of oblivion
Morning stillness restored

# Tea Two

Danny O'Connor

Jist aboot the furst thing we boat when we wur furst merit wis a china tea set. Hud tae huv wan fur when hur mother came oan a Sunday didn't we?

Nen she goat smashed an smashed all that fuckin china didn't she? Bit it wis mah fault wisn't it? Ah made hur do it didn't ah? Ah don't remember zactly whit it wis ah did tae make hur dae it bit hur memory's better than mine isn't it? An she says ah made hur dae it so ah must've mustn't ah? Cos efter aw, ahm a man n she's a wuman irin't we?

Aw them early years we never hud money fur oany mair china did we? So it wis mugs o tea that hur mother turned hur nose up at didn't she? Didn't matter hoo hard ah boilt the kettle, hoo much mulk ah pit in, did i? Level spoons or heaped, it didnae matter did it? Marks-n-Spencer tea bags n aw. Bit hur mother's nose never retreatit doon frae the vertical did it?

As ah said, them early years, we hid plenty weans, plenty fights, plenty empty boatels, bit nae china did we? Wisn't tae wan night years, later she trumps 'Ahm away tae the A.A.' that the penny drapt didn't it? It wis quite a while efter it, bit wan day she brought hame a big smile didn't she? An under her erm wis a case o best ming china wisn't it?

# Haiku

Catherine Baird

An open novel
Dust gathered in middle pages
When will you come back?

# Weighty Problem

J. B. Quinn

Counting calories
Measuring portions
Weighing flesh
Subtracting fat
Exchanging recipes
Calculating steps
Financing fees
Paying cost
Mounting hunger
Decreasing commitment
Expanding waistline
Adding pounds
Doubling effort
Multiplying temptation
Dividing resistance
Diminishing returns
Playing the numbers game
Failed the chocolate exam
Again!

# UK History: Learning From Our Ancestors. Part 1 of 299; The Glasgow Tongs (2043-2044)

James A. Stewart

In trying to understand our present it is imperative we learn from the mistakes of the past. It is easy to forget it was only forty years ago, in 2043, when the Tongs had full control of the fair city of Glasgow, so renamed in 2045. The mission behind the *Learning From Our Ancestors* series of papers is to bring to life our history and to educate today's youth on how Scotland came to be the worldly unique nation that it is today.

In Part 1, I will give a brief overview as to how the Glasgow Tongs came to power and will touch on some of the policies of the short-lived Tongian authority. Secondly, this paper carries in its latter pages the shortened minutes of a Tongian Council meeting dealing with the agreement and implementation of a scheme to define Tongian corporal punishment, and to clarify the reasons for which physical penance was to be meted out to offenders. This was the start-up meeting for the initiative which was officially known as 'Project Scud'.

This short paper is intended only to be an introduction to the Tongs and should not be regarded as an exhaustive study into the gang. Later editions of *Learning From Our Ancestors* will give further insight into the much heralded Glaswegian gang and will build upon the overview which follows here. For further and in-depth analysis of the Tongian phenomenon I heartily recommend Percival Postlethwaite's seminal work *Tongs: Cracked Heads and Balls, The Definitive History of Electoral Opportunism and Madcap Ministrations.*

By 2041 the people of Glasgow had become so disillusioned with politics that the turnout for Glasgow council elections was a record low of only 1.2%[1]. All of the votes were for the Tongs Ya Bass Party, save one. The exception was a vote for the Ghost of Tommy Sheridan Party, Ms Kane of Glasgow later revealed she voted for the GTSP by mistake citing her worsening Alzheimer's as the reason for her slip of the pen.[2]

But how did what amounted to a 'gang' get to take charge of Scotland's largest council? The catalyst was the collapse of the two major banking institutions in the early part of the twenty-first century. RBS [Royal Bank of Scotland] and BOS [plain old Bank of Scotland] were symbols of the original Scottish Enlightenment. These old institutions epitomised the days when Scots were at the forefront of world thinking and innovation. Over hundreds of years the banks delivered unmatched resources into the treasury of Great Britain and then latterly the United Kingdom. When the collapse started there was some quite significant vitriol aimed at the Banks, and Scotland, over the value of the support being given to them. King described them as "parasitical leeches hell-bent on the

---

1 *The Sun Newspaper;* (June 15, 2041 pg 3): The model's left nipple was used as a decimal point.

2 The Memoirs of Rosie Kane: A Skint Socialist Sells-out (2044, pg. 201) – *Ms. R. Kane*

collapse of the UK Treasury."[3] In the end, after trillions of pounds in support, both banks collapsed during the fourth credit crunch of the 21st century, in the mid-2030s. England had had enough and, in an emergency referendum, voted to give Scotland independence.[4] This was despite the protestations of Alex Salmond, who by this stage was so senile he believed he was possessed by the ghost of Winston Churchill. [5]

Coincidentally, and some argued at the time rather conveniently, the last of the North Sea oil had been drilled. The platforms closed down and Scotland was left with only one reasonable opportunity for income: tourism. In keeping with the malaise and run of back luck the country was having, the midge, now extinct, had developed immunity to Ovan's *Skin Sore Soft*[6]. This was a catastrophic mutation and one which meant most tourists only came to Scotland once, if at all. Photographer Kier Gray's most famous portrait of a pockmarked American tourist[7] was described by Hamish McCrae, "as having done the most damage to the Scottish tourist industry since Queen Elizabeth tasted Haggis."[8]

The people of Scotland's cities were apathetic but in the rural areas votes were cast to revert to a feudal system of land management. The great clans rose again; the McDonalds and Campbells had a bloody and year-long battle to settle old scores and some new clans fought their

---

3 A Considered View on the Credit Crunch (2011, pg. 22) – *Mr M. King*

4 Why Scots are Celts, Not Brits (2036, pg. 1-200) – *Mr A. Brons*

5 Fxxx-off and Take Your Pound Notes With You (2037, pg. 1-300) – *Mr N. Griffin*

6 The Beastie Bites Back (2031, pg. 39) – *Dr. M. Ure*

7 Reflections on a Scottish Hiking Holiday (2036, pg. 102) – *Mr. K. Gray*

8 Smoke Cigars and the Midge Will Stay Away (2037, pg. 1) – *Mr H. McCrae*

way to the top-table; including the Ahmeds as well as the vicious and power-hungry Podolskis.[9]

Back in the cities, of which only Glasgow, Edinburgh and Aberdeen could be regarded as such, there were some attempts made to retain government in a social democratic manner. Aberdeen's aspirations were ended when the sea-levels rose overnight after a freak meteorite landed in the Arctic, and as a consequence the Granite City disappeared under water. Dundee had been lost in the 2030s when a rather vicious Poet Laureate, in a fit of pique at the new found popularity of Sir William McGonagall, detonated a nuclear bomb in the city. It was speculated in some quarters that it was McGonagall's posthumous knighthood from Queen Beatrice that was the tipping point for Mr Fry's sanity.[10]

Edinburgh was conquered by the Irish who saw her potential as a tourist magnet and they built a tunnel direct from Dublin to the former Scots capital. The castle was re-painted in resplendent green, white and gold and a giant novelty Guinness hat was placed over the rather ugly barracks to take the sting out of its architectural awfulness. Drink was re-priced as Edinburgh was one of the few places in the world more expensive than Dublin for alcohol.[11]

By the time of the 2041 elections, Glasgow was the only Scottish city to hold a vote as the remainder of the country's population simply didn't care. The Glasgow election was the first in Scotland for five years and as well as having a population made up of 95% alcoholics[12] (the

---

9 A Scottish Clan History (2067, pg 187-209) – *Dr. H. McCrae*

10 What Happened to Scotland's Cities? (2068, pg. 517-608) – *Dr. H. McCrae*

11 The Building of O'Edinburgh (2040) – *Mr C. O'Doherty*

12 Source: 2041 census of population.

remaining 5% declared medically comatose), the bankrupt Glasgow authority relied on local groups to spread the news of the election. On reviewing how the Tongs got in, Percival Postlethwaite cited a chain of avoidable events which led to the gang's election.[13] The first of these mistakes was when the distribution of the leaflets was given to John McMalky, and in classic Glasgow delivery boy fashion he put them in the bin; but not before his prison educated father saw them. McMalky Snr mobilised the Tongs, took leadership of the gang/party and stood for local government. Thanks to his son's laziness, the Tongs leader was elected with the overwhelming majority outlined earlier. When the Tongs came to power 98.8% of people were not even aware there had been an election.

The leader of the Tongs, Malky McMalky, decreed martial law would be implemented and a new series of by-laws were to be passed to rid the streets of suit wearers, those who refused to wear a baseball cap at the prescribed angle and to close any shops which McMalky deemed to be 'posh'. The exceptions to these rules were those who sold Tongian approved apparel, such as the classic clothing companies of Burberry and Kappa and the tool supplier to the Tongs, Victor Morris. Irn-Bru was given free to all school-children and religious education was amended to incorporate football club affiliation. Atheists had the right to chose between Queen's Park and Partick Thistle. Lapsed or not, Catholics had to follow Celtic whilst Protestants were forced to wear the red, white and blue of Rangers. The sectarian songs outlawed in the noughties were brought back with a renewed vigour. The Tongian philosophy was simple and their mission statement read; 'The imposition of

---

13 Tongs: Cracked Heads and Balls, The Definitive History of Electoral Opportunism and Madcap Ministrations (2051) – *Mr. P. Postlethwaite*

corporal punishment is only possible by encouraging lawlessness'.[14]

Many of the policies of the previous regime remained in place. McMalky's belief was that it "if it is broke then don't fix it".[15] Taxes were levied on luxury goods like fruit, vegetables and wine (excluding tonic and other such high strength alcoholic drinks loosely termed as wine) as well as clothing which couldn't be regarded as part of the Tongian uniform. Denims, ties, any footwear not pure white, and woolly hats all fell victim to this tax. Within a year, eighty percent of all clothing sold in Tongland [the name Glasgow carried under Tongian rule] was made from recycled shell and track suits.

The Tongs came to power with a whimper and no resistance. In the course of their internship the Tongs were responsible for some of the most bizarre and ludicrous policies Britain had seen since the now derided New Labour government elected in 1997. Despite fierce criticism over the last few decades, the Tongians are widely regarded as being the catalyst for bringing the UK back together and the subsequent re-colonisation of much of the Commonwealth. They can be rightly chided for their approach to office but we have them to thank for reminding us how important fascism is as a control mechanism.

This paper is intended to provide an introduction to the conditions from which such a regime could rise and should the reader wish to find out more about the Tongs, the *Learning From Our Ancestors* programme includes some twenty parts dedicated to them including a profile of Malky McMalky, a review of the battle plan for the ill fated

---

14 We're In Charge, Ya Bass: The First Tong's Press Release (2041) – *Mr. M. McMalky*

15 Looking Back (2044) – *Sir M. McMalky*

War of Ambition when McMalky lead the Tongs against both the Sharks and the Jets at the same time and a piece dedicated to the fall of the Tongian Empire. In the meantime, the following minutes will give the reader an appreciation of how the Tongs found themselves caught between trying to create a plausible bureaucracy and their general wish to implement social disorder and to continually carry out the ministration of pain.

**Project Scud**

*The following is an appended excerpt from the minutes of the Project Scud kick-off meeting. The language has been changed from Tong-Scots-English back into English for ease of reading. The verbatim minutes are available on request.*

**Attendees: Malky McMalky (MM), Kev Knifer (KK), Al Asbo (AA), Def Freat (DF), Trout (T), Jamo (J), Des (D), Boab (B)**

**Agenda:**
1. Aims of Project Scud
2. Scope
3. Roll-out strategy
4. Next steps

**1. Aims**

The aim of Project Scud is to provide the citizens of Tongland, man, with some unclear guidelines of what is, and what isn't, acceptable behaviour. Know.

**2. Scope**

All citizens of Tongland are in scope for Project Scud. Initially Project Scud will launch in Bearsden due to the rich pickings there for some of the proposed measures. In scope are all laws, current and future, all citizens (except the McMalky family) and visitors to Tongland must accept these rules also and will be handed a copy upon arrival at any of the city checkpoints. Right?

It is proposed we implement corporal punishment for the following offences:

- Wearing a suit (except for court appearances)
- Getting good marks at school
- Conversing in public without a nasal whine
- Conversing in private without a nasal whine
- Refusal to engage in public disorder
- Not meeting the requisite number of underage liaisons
- Feeling the posterior of someone's girlfriend, unless both parties are inebriated
- And anything else which irks the Tongland council; like long hair for example

To avoid ambiguity, corporal punishment is regarded as a kick in the groin area, the number of said kicks will increase exponentially with the frequency and severity of the offence.

### 3. Roll-out Strategy

It is proposed we pilot Project Scud in Bearsden and then roll-out to Milngavie within one week and other former posh areas to follow immediately thereafter (Newton Mearns, West End, etc). In respect to communications, there are no plans to issue any. It has been agreed by the Council that forewarning people will only take away from the impact of Project Scud. The Tongian mantra of 'there is no lesson like a [physically] painful one' applies to Project

Scud. Upon full roll-out it is expected we will need three thousand NEDS (Necessary Enforcement Disciples) to execute the full range of punitive measures coming out of Project Scud.

**4. Next Steps**

Implement ASAP and start kicking balls. The following project team will lead Project Scud into implementation:

Lead Project Manager: Al Asbo
Implementation Manager: Trout
Design, Build and Test: Des
Benefits Delivery: Def Threat

**Conclusion**

In this introductory paper we were given an insight into how the Tongs got to take office in Glasgow. We got a feel for how they set about organising themselves. In addition, despite their much maligned government, the Tongs provided much to ponder for the clans and feudal rulers of Scotland at the time. The gang had been opportunist and brutal. Their ascension to power proved to be the catalyst for much change in Scotland. Gone were niceties such as democracy, equal rights and socialism. In their place came punitive measures for inane incidents, prescriptive education and totalitarian ideals.

These principles remain true to this day. We are great nation for them, the greatest in the world. Our leader is all powerful and thanks to his greatness you are allowed to learn our past and savour the events which shaped our great nation.

## Freedom of Speech

Erin McHugh

Long, long ago, we fought, we sought
The power to speak without inhibition
Won our deserved civil liberties, we thought
But it seems now the government's on its own little mission
To stifle our cries of injustice and protest
Distract us with scare tactics to help us digest
The controlled terror threatening us daily
While the state slowly and surely takes our rights away
Freedom of speech is now long gone
Demonstrate outside Parliament and police will arrest you
Headlines of bomb factories are just a con
Left violated but the real terrorists say you can't sue
Detained without charge for up to 28 days
Age old right of habeas corpus stolen away
We the 51st state collude to torture our fellow man
While our leaders destroy what we fought for as quietly as
they can
Cling on to your freedom and see the irony
Of Bush and Blair's Nobel peace nomination and the BNP
For as long as we fear them, tyrants will rule
We need to claim back what's ours and revolt against their
bull

# Uplifting

William N. Dyer

I've just been lifted by the police. They say that I'm a suspected terrorist. Me! I couldn't hurt a fly.

They're taking me up to Pitt Street Police Station. It's where they do all the anti-terrorist stuff.

The handcuffs are hurting like a hot iron on bare flesh. They've got me in a car. We're speeding along the A80 towards Glasgow, and I mean speeding. Who says that there's only one law?

Who would play a crazy joke on me? It's got to be someone from the office. I don't remember crossing anyone, in the office or anywhere else for that matter. What the hell's going on?

Perhaps it's one of those stupid reality TV shows. The docudramas or candid camera crap. I've often wondered what sad souls watch that type of cheap rubbish. And they think I'm a threat to this country and culture.

The car smells of stale sweat, urine and fear. That's what that third smell must be. Nobody says a word to me. There is only the chatter of the radio. There are four policemen in the car. Two in the front and one either side of me in the rear. All nice and cosy.

They really do that thing with your head when they put you in the car. You know, the hand on top of your head to stop you from bumping it and accusing them of police brutality. What they're doing is brutal as far as I feel right now. This has got to be a joke.

I feel every bump on the road. We have rubbish roads. We put up with a lot of crap in this country. And we end up being screwed. This has got to be a gag or a mistake. For God's sake. Why is this happening to me?

As we approach the outskirts of Glasgow they put on the siren. The lights had been flashing when the car had left my house. You see the rubber-neckers trying to get an eye-full of the criminal in the black and white. But in this country, the cars, unlike everything else, aren't black and white.

We're just joining the M8 at the old gasometer. The mood of the police in the car is changing to one of expectancy. I'm not sure what it had been on the way in. Maybe it's me that's feeling expectant and I am just transferring my feelings to them.

We're coming off at the Charing Cross exit. We'll be at the station in a couple of minutes depending on the traffic flow.

The car's getting very warm. The sweat is running down my brow. My heart is pounding and my head is throbbing. My breathing is laboured.

The car screeches to a stop. The street's empty.

Why did the driver grind to a halt? He must really have liked that effect.

The front passenger gets out to open the rear near-side door. I didn't realise that they used the childproof locks.

# Brigadoon in Banffshire

Eddie McGonnell

They say you appear only once
In one hundred years
from your mist-enshrouded slumber.
As I watch the wild North Sea
Batter your whitewashed houses,
I want to step back into the picture
Of that magical dance with time.
Crovie!
Your cliff-face hangs over you
Like some benign, protective shield,
Reluctant to allow grasping strangers
Their pursuit of your age-old secret.
That splash of red
Against the white of angry rollers,
Was daubed with Monet-like perception.
A phonebox, that seems out of place,
Retains a quiet dignity.
The ghosts of time
Have chosen your sleepy harbour
With Gaelic wisdom.
That coastal path wends its way across your face
Like some winding ribbon of quietness

To where lovers once walked,
And shared secrets.
Crovie!
I want so much to stay with you;
To enjoy the tranquil heaven
Of knowing
Your quiet, time-worn secret.

# Nothing

Catherine Baird

Way up high where the rays are
the show starts and I am amused,
feel the lift
feel my ribs expand and shake my hair out in the breeze
Laugh until my trachea
aches
and the pain is like my swallowing muscles
hammered into submission.
Drug myself to escape this pain and
drug myself again to escape the guilt of drugs
when I ought to know that
god, some god of a sort
will relieve this pain if only
I can learn to endure
if only I could hold off,
let the pain course through
and expect its relief as I was taught.
I laugh again.
De nada.

# Target

J. B. Quinn

There's been another murder!
Looks like the body was bludgeoned to death
Then re-arranged to look like natural causes
The deceased leaves behind many dependents
And will be sorely missed by millions
As they struggle on alone and desolate
Although it was common knowledge
That the victim was being stalked
By a particularly vicious adversary
Corrupt political practise prevents investigation
As the bereaved come to terms with their loss
The authorities maintain death was inevitable

There's been another murder!
The remains of Socialism will be cremated
For fear that burial may lead to resurrection.

# The Hipness Crown

Danny O'Connor

Wee Garry was the hippest hippy who jangled his beads on our stretch of the A8 from Muirhead in the west to Moodiesburn in the east and the dogleg to Timber Town. Places like Annathill and Twechar were a century or more behind any idea of anything other than fortified wine and rotgut whisky. He was not just for the weekend; his hipness was 24*7 with a dash of 60*60 for good measure.

Garry's best pal, Riddo, Ridd or El Ridd, depending on the swing of his mood, was always up there with Garry. But Ridd had a streak of meanness that had been fertilized, nurtured and grown-on since kicking his way out of the womb, which barred him from ever settling in any peace camp. In a later epoch he found God and Redemption - but that's another story: the story of El Ridd.

Garry stood some five feet-two off the ground but he punched the weight of a much bigger bloke. From '68 to '74 he clad himself entirely in blue denim and his long, lank hair was so black that it hurt your eyes just to look at it. If it was pharmaceutical, the bold Garry took it. Toked: *Mary Jane* in '68, *Paki Black* in '69, *Lebanese Red* in '70, and any old shit thereafter. He dropped acid as quick as the silver medallist weightlifter in the super-heavyweight contest dropped that last unattainable golden weight. Blue, red, paper or jellybean. They all scurried down Garry's throat on the journey to open his mind to the limitlessness of the yin and the loftiness counterpoint of the yang. It also froze his wang as a sort of celibate penance for all those metaphysical ponderings. He sped on speed, eyeballs as bright as a pinball, darting left, darting right, forever darting but never quite seeing the paranoia rushing full-tilt-boogie up from behind. Coke was a joke. He snorted so much of the stuff that, one day, when he was communing with nature, every scintilla of mucus membrane dropped out from his nose like a placenta into the Luggie burn. To wash out of his life forever.

Wee Garry's specialty was the 'Festival Weekender'. He and Riddo would bum their way down to whatever music festival was on. Isle of Wight, Reading, it didn't matter. Garry and Ridd would be there. Ridd and Garry together. Because 'being there' was not just important - it was all. One pair of bolt cutters later, they were through the security fence and heading for their fix. Garry had this way of knowing without knowing who were the police narks, the con-artists and the genuine one hundred percent purveyors of temporary nirvana. The 'Weekender' consisted of a speedball laced with acid (lysergic s d to you and I), and god knows what else. Warfarin or some such rat killer.

The object was to get you high (speed) and keep you high (acid) for the two to three day's duration of the festival without ever coming down, without the need for anything else except maybe an optional three bottles of vodka and half-a-dozen special brews, pre-purchased and nestling out of temptation's way at the bottom of a rolled-up sleeping bag. If he ever felt himself coming off a high,

Garry would badger his supplier for another tab, free gratis or else he would let the cognoscenti know the man's produce didn't cut it. Someone of Garry's repute rubbishing his wares would be the kiss of death in the volatile and shifting market of a pop festival.

Getting high and staying high; that's what made Garry King of the Weekenders.

In those days, even Garry had limits. If you couldn't sniff it, smoke it, pour it or do it orally, he wasn't interested. Horse was an animal never ridden. Neither bareback in a joint nor reined and saddled in a spoon and needle.

Garry was always first to know what bands were in and what bands were out. He only had to have an album cover under his arm once and all his acolytes in our cosy little world back in those Days of Innocence would be carrying it under their arms in a trice. Some would even go as far as buying the album and actually playing it in the hope that their opinion might one day be canvassed. The rest merely nicked the cover out of the music shop and tucked it under their arm just to look cool.

Before Riddo (almost rhymes with Psycho and Sicko) bested the fates by becoming an almost-hippy, they had a career plan all laid out for him. Back in the mid-sixties, before he dropped acid, Riddo was your prototype callow youth. In the U S of A, he would have been a juvenile delinquent. But they had not been invented here in those days. *Rotten Apple No. 1* was old Balderdash, his head teacher's (primary school) description of him. Both he and *Petty Larceny* were always in and out of each other's pockets. It was only a matter of time, old Balderdash kept repeating, before the boy Riddo would be sent to an approved school to start his true life's education. Then it would be Jail, Glasgow and Gangsterism in that order.

Old Balderdash had a sort of pride in his past pupils. When the playground was quiet and Mrs McGuire (who peed in the fire, you know) had paused from battering religion and hymns into her poor charges, old B would daydream Riddo's life away. He had El Ridd through approved school and two jail terms in double quick time. Old B now had our Ridd teaming up with a jailbird pal and becoming first an enforcer, and then a minor czar in Glasgow's gangland, in charge of gambling or prostitution, before reaching his mid-forties when he would grow fat and lazy before being kneecapped out of the business by the local lodge of the Red Hand of Ulster to finance their just war against the Taigs of which, because of his schooling, El Ridd numbered as one.

Eddie, The Pretender, tried hard to match Garry and El Ridd in the hipness stakes. He was desperate to make up the third in the holy triumvirate of cool. Just like the Father, Son and Holy Ghost. Any deaf, dumb and blind kid could be guided to his Timber Town door by the earth tremors created by his playing of Led Zeppelin II at a zillion decibels as soon as his dad left for work.

Eddie was sucked into the drug scene like a baby reaching for his mother's nipple. Not content with the user end of the supply-chain, Eddie began by peddling tiny deals to the terminally naive and the first-time dabblers. So he was, in effect, getting his drugs for free. His first scam was to buy a quarter of Paki Black and then sell on an eighth for his cost price, to the great uninitiated. As I said: drugs for free.

Soon, Eddie was connected further and further up the chain until introduced to a real-live Glasgow gang boss, all razor scars and sharkskin suit. He told Eddie how he liked the cut of his gib and put him on commission. After a while Eddie thought he knew enough to go independent. Eddie was a tough boy; we all gave him that. He was also a bit thick. Thickness or bravado? We never knew. Anyway, for whatever reason, he ignored his first warning - an ordinary sort of bruising, nothing that would stop him hustling, you understand. So, he carried on regardless. Unperturbed, the sharkskin suit had Eddie taken from his then abode, in Drumchapel, far from our cosy section of the A8. Eddie The Pretender got his face blown off with a shotgun and his hands chopped from his wrists with a blunt hatchet. We never did find out which came first, the hatchet or the shotgun.

After the unlamented demise of Eddie, it was not until Punk raised its repulsive persona that anyone emerged with a strong enough constitution to challenge Garry and Ridd in the consumption of pharmaceuticals. The challenge came not from one of Garry's many acolytes but unexpectedly, upstream from our section of the A8, in Stepps. And not from a punk but from a genuine third-generation weekend hippy. A fellow known to us all as Bobo's Boy. He was a devotee of those German weird-outs, Amon Dull II.

The concept of Peace and Love never bedded-in to Bobo's Boy's persona. He was a plain arriviste with all the finer feeling of a trashcan rodent. On the day he declared his independence by modifying his father's features with those youthful six-feet-two sized fists, he started to grow that crazy, tight-curled, Hendrix hair of his. We were not impressed. To us, he was still Bobo's Boy. Pummelling an old man with a bad heart, who was a good head-and-a-bit smaller than you, did not strike us as a class act - even if the old bastard was your da. Anyway his independence did not extend as far as leaving home. His mother's apron strings were bound far too tight for that. Remember, he was only a weekend hippy after all. Not the genuine 365 carat that was Wee Garry. Plus, Bobo's Boy carried his toady wee pal around with him everywhere, just to hear someone tell him how wonderful he was. Toady was even more of a repulsive nerd than Bobo's Boy, so we all blamed Bobo's Boy for inflicting the wee shite on us.

The time I'm talking about was when a Moog synthesiser was de rigueur for any band with pretensions. In the infancy of the Moog they had this cachet of mystery about them. No one quite knew what they were. They were also bloody expensive. Bobo's Boy claimed he could make one cheap. A local band let him hang out on the basis of that claim but he turned out so nerdy that they just used him as a sort of verbal punch-bag. It was by being associated with this band that Bobo's Boy gained some credibility with the easily bedazzled. He also gained access to the band's cornucopia of drugs.

The sound of London calling me meant that I never did find out what all that acid did to Bobo's Boy's few marbles or if he ever did get round to making that Moog... but that's two whole other stories.

# My World Was Full of Darkness

Craig Murray

My world was full of Darkness
My life was going nowhere
And I couldn't care less
Spending my days risking my health
Paying to slowly kill myself
I thought I'd never lose control
No one ever does
I thought it was just a bit of fun
I didn't want to hurt anyone

## No Fixed Abode

Eddie McGonnell

Their cardboard haven
Has all the permanency
Of snow on a summer's day.
Their ragged, dirty attire
Suggests that they are beggars
These men, however, are alive with dignity,
And cultivate a quiet friendship
That shocks the senses
With its measured sincerity.

As each day dawns,
Painful truths are faced.
The endless trekking around the city
Wearies them.
But society has to be made aware
That their outstretched hands
Are rifling the conscience
Of the establishment.

Of course it's their own fault
That they are poor.
With their dirt and squalor

They don't deserve to mingle with decent people.
Best to hush them with a Judas pence,
Best to condemn them
To a life of misery,
Than plant a daffodil
In the weed-filled garden
Of human indifference.

# Broken

J. B. Quinn

Bones crack
Under the crushing blow of control
A lifetime of silent screams
Held prisoner by fear
One by one the broken pieces fall:
Broken ribs
Broken jaw
Broken wrist
Broken heart
Broken trust
Broken down
Into their constituent parts

Now the spell has broken
Now the fear has ended
All the broken pieces
Can be gathered up and mended

Love cracks
Under the rising pressure of outrage
A lifetime of silence - screams
Held prisoner by need

One by one the broken pieces fall:
Broken sleep
Broken promises
Broken dreams
Broken home
Broken up
Broken down
Into their constituent parts

Now the silence has broken
Now the need has ended
All the broken pieces
Can be gathered up and mended

# Show Me A Funny Comedian And I'll Show You A Certifiable Madman

James A. Stewart

I try to avoid their eyes when I speak. Their stares burn right through me: I feel as though my forehead is on fire as fifty-odd eyes gawk at me as I prepare myself here on this petite stage. I say fifty-odd as one of them is blind and another is wearing an eye-patch under her glasses, so I can't be sure of the exact number of eyes.

I stand in front of them. I have the microphone and the resulting power which comes from being the person able to shout loudest in a crowd. My uniform is a bit messy, but in the dimmed lights of the hall they won't be able to see any marks. It was ironed nice. The creases on my trousers are razor sharp, just like my wit.

This is my big moment. I have been building up to this. It needs to be a success as I may never get another chance at it. I have been practising in front of a mirror every day. My lines, my actions and even my facial expressions have all been perfected. In the last fortnight I have tried out my art on unsuspecting members of the public with limited success, hence the insecurity.

I am nervous as the sweat on my palms causes the microphone to slip slightly. I fumble to catch it but the thuds and thumps that resonate through the PA system sounds like a giant running down the hallway. I glance up into the void; the apprehension is clear on my face.

Through the spotlight I see a couple of malicious grins, and I know those are directed at me. There is a woman, her hands behind her back, with tears rolling down her cheeks. Am I that funny? A man gives her a hug and kisses the top of her head. People come and go from time to time: I guess to the toilet, I don't get involved. It's simply not worth the hassle and at the end of the day it's what assistants are for. I need to keep my focus.

Most people look ahead. They don't know whether to laugh or cry. My preparations are complete. Keeping my composure and imposing my style on this audience is going to be my biggest challenge yet. I have first night nerves and it shows.

I tell my opening joke. No applause, which is understandable. I try for my next one, it's a beauty. I lower my head to the microphone, "I asked the teacher if she would punish me for something I didn't do. 'Of course not,' she said. 'Phew,' I replied, ''cos I haven't done my homework.'" I get nothing. This audience is tough.

Next up I try a joke ripped off from Ellen DeGeneris. "You have to stay in shape. My grandmother started walking five miles a day when she was sixty. She's ninety seven today and we don't know where the hell she is." I get a slight murmur of approval from a girl to the left, but I don't know if it is because she recognises the joke or approves of my delivery. I make a mental note not to tell any more recycled jokes.

I move onto my favourite story about the time when I lost my virginity. Only, if you could see me you'd know it could never be true. Silence again.

I shout into the microphone, "LAUGH YOU BASTARDS."

Near the back, a child howls, I hate children laughing more than anything. I guess by doing my first gig in a school assembly hall I run the risk of having kids there. They laugh at the most mundane things and their laughter can be so cruel. The innocence of mirth, huh! So what if I have a limp? It is not funny. Yes, I have a birthmark on my face but that doesn't mean I should be pointed at, laughed at or mocked. I am a person, too.

The crying woman at the front wails some more. She's not enjoying the show. Her blonde hair falls in front of her eyes and she flicks her head in response.

I can make people laugh just by being there. I am poked at, prodded and bullied because I am 'different'. Who cares if I am not able to make the football team, or am in the special science classes in case I injure someone else? I am me. I deserve to be treated the same. I want people to laugh with me, not at me. I am funny, I know I am. Before my mum died she used to say that I was the funniest little boy in the world.

I consider asking my assistant, Joe, to untie the audience's hands. Maybe if they can relax and applaud they'll enjoy the show more. He looks over as if he can read my mind and shakes his head, and motions for me to get on with the show. I tell a blonde joke I had memorised, one I got off the internet. The blonde woman, my English teacher, shouts out. "Aaron. Let us go. This is madness."

"Are you heckling me, Miss Smith?" I ask through the mic, the menace in my voice apparent.

"No, God, No." She says, but it is too late. I have already raised the gun.

"I deal with hecklers the way Elvis dealt with poor TV shows." The speed at which her head whips back is eerie. The child's howls from earlier come at me twenty-times over. Joe makes a b-line for the exit. He knows I have begun my encore early. Screams fill the room as I level my gun again.

The doors on either side of the assembly hall burst open. Joe is gunned down, and the SWAT team train their guns on me. I'm done for. As the bullets come tearing through the air toward me, I realise that a forced audience will neither laugh at or with you. I have failed.

# How the West Has Won

J. B. Quinn

Grasping greed
Plants its seed
No war on want, make them bleed

Free trade free-for-all
Survival of the best?
Existence scratched out for the rest

Sweatshop labour
Make them pay
Life is cheap on a dollar a day

Deeply indebted
Trapped by mean philosophy
Hell on earth living in poverty

Short-changed lives
Counting the cost
Corporations count profit and loss

Foreign aid
Bitter pill prescribed
Sickness continues when health's denied

Worked to death
Shallow graves dug deep
Millions piled high on a new scrap heap

Rapacious hands grab
Every precious grain of soil
Wringing out every rich drop of oil

Profit margins' high excess
Old imperialism's new kingdom come
Enslaving nations: how the West has won.

# The Eglinton Electreum

Eddie McGonnell

John Wayne rode across the prairies
And covered wagons forded swollen streams
While we booed and cheered in the Eglinton Electreum.
For threepence we were inducted every Saturday
Into a magical world of cowboy opera.
Where we argued as to who was the best fighter
Between Hopalong Cassidy and Johnny Mack Brown
And did Gabby Hayes ever have a black beard.

The ice cream woman was met
By a thunderous posse of parched prospectors
Fighting to pay for a half-chocolate ice.
Slider Broon, whom I always envied,
Sat with his gang quite brazenly,
Smoking Wild Woodbine cigarettes,
Watching the smoke spiralling ever upwards
To Arizona skies.

The magic box would occasionally break down:
I remember once, in the middle of an attack
On the stagecoach by the Apaches.
How the audacity of the fumbling, bumbling projectionist

Was greeted by howls of derision,
And orange peel and apple stumps were thrown
At the silver screen.
Who was scared of the Apaches anyway?

Girls were banned as being soppy.
This was a macho matinee.
Kisses were for cissies
And any girl brave enough
To confront the Saturday desperadoes
Was confined to the back-seats,
Where Calamity Jane
Sang "Secret Love".

Legends were born
And moving pictures believed.
And boyhood camaraderie was given credence,
In the Electreum;
In the Gorbals;
Under cover of darkness.

# Sell Out

J. B. Quinn

Buy, buy, buy
Beg, steal or borrow
Sell, sell, sell
Everything must go

Buy, buy, buy
A lifestyle then extend it
Sell, sell, sell
Give or take the credit

Buy, buy, buy
On the never-never and beyond
Sell, sell, sell
Pipe dreams of a hyped-up wonderland

Buy, buy, buy
All hopes and fears, each smile and frown
Sell, sell, sell
Anything and everything not nailed down

Buy, buy, buy
Up the whole market place

Sell, sell, sell
Before or on the sell-by-date

Buy, buy, buy
Until economies of scale cease
Sell, sell, sell
Until diminishing returns increase

Buy, buy, buy
Another cliché; every line in the book
Sell, sell, sell
Liberally sprinkled lies; economise the truth

Buy, buy, buy
More time; as long as it lasts
Sell, sell, sell
Every second of the future, present, past

Buy, buy, buy
Whatever the cost, leave not a trace
Sell, sell, sell
Yourself: sell out the human race

Buy, buy, buy
The whole world and all within it
Then stop…
Until I get off, then repackage and re-spin it.

# Wake Up

Danny O'Connor

'Wakey, wakey. Rise and shine. Get up. Get out of the pine'

'C'mon Danny-boy. Time to get up. Time to do a poo and a pee-pee too.'

Dan heard the cajolement right in the centre of his brain. As his consciousness swam ever upwards from the darkest depths of the induced cryo-sleep the returning sentience was becoming awash with the flotsam and jetsam of senses and emotions that made the transition from the chemically induced nirvana dream state where he was literally a God-in-his-Own-Universe to the ordinary reality of his human existence, a convoluted confection of confusion where he was still unable to separate his cryogenic-cradle existence from real-time reality.

The robotic edge to the billing and cooing that was teasing him out of his omnipotence and into the frailty of normalcy was having the calculated desired effect on his synapses. He felt the onrush of adrenalin pressure-wash the torpor from his mind.

If it truly was the voice of the onboard computer arousing him untimely from the programmed centuries-long stasis death that was cryogenic sleep then that meant one of two situations and both of them were bad.

If the robotic dissonance in the vowels was only the machinations of the dream-time segment of his artificial sleep then the back of his mind reassured him that, despite all evidence to the contrary, he was not, in point of fact, in any mortal danger. His only problem then was that he was fixed on the spigot of not knowing which was which. Not only that but he was also speared on the conundrum that he had no method of divining the continuing but ultimately safe dream from perilous reality.

It was at this point that his training kicked in. His synesthetic learning showed the wording of this section of the manual in deep and dangerous red. Not only that but the very words contained in his mind's eye were howling a high pitched alarm and the smell from them was by turns both acrid and sanguine. This deliberate overloading of his senses produced the desired effect of bringing him into fully functioning wakefulness at a speed faster than light, faster also than the ship's motive power at full tilt.

The arcane word 'engines' flickered through his ocular synapses in bad, crackling neon just to emphasise his danger for the same pedantic purpose that the ponderous defence programme in the manual was over-egging the pudding of his current dilemma. Because of course, the ship had no engines in the sense of mechanized motive power just as the craft taking him to his destination was not a 'ship' in the sense of a transport as in the history archives. Just, also, as he, when he awoke, would not have a corporeal 'body' in the sense of two arms, two legs and a torso. No, personkind had evolved away from that kind of nonsense. So far in fact, that many, like he himself, refused to believe in those old myths and abandoned them as they abandoned the comfort blanket when they left the confines of the kindergarten.

Be his condition a dream or reality the training manual dictated that he treat it as though it were real. So he visioned himself surfacing out from the depths of a rock pool in an enchanted sun-kissed island of outstanding natural beauty and there to greet him holding a voluptuous bath towel was his equally beautiful and equally voluptuous and ever-willing partner whose sad-eyed smile echoed the depths of her loneliness and longing for him.

The fabrications of the manual sure beat the racking reality of expulsion from cryo-sleep.

# Reasons Not to Marry: No. 1

James A. Stewart

Paige Khan and Jerry Turner held hands
and ran, and ran, and ran. They laughed
and giggled and swigged from same bottle.

I love you, Paige.
I know, Jerry.

Paige kissed Jerry's cheek and he felt her
tight buttocks, she feigned shock and
pushed him away.

You're a rascal, Jerry.
I know, Paige.

The sun settled into darkness and the sparks
from their dying barbecue shot up into the
starry sky.

Let's get married, Paige.
We can't, Jerry. People would call me a good
book; and you take my name? No.

You're right again, Paige. I guess we'll just
continue this life of god-mocking infidelity
instead. They kissed.

# The Renegade

Samuel McCann

Firelight illuminated the weathered features of the sorry-looking individuals crowding around the blazing oil-drum. The run-down back streets of New York City in winter were an unforgiving place, especially at night, and the people who dwelled here were the dregs of society, gathering in the shadows around whatever warmth was afforded them far from society's judging eyes. Events of late had forced them to huddle even closer together on the fear-haunted streets as a brood of vicious thrill-seekers roamed abroad, striking terror into their hearts.

Even as a score of them basked in the glow of a single drum, they became alerted to the dazzling lights of an oncoming vehicle and were forced to scatter as it tore through their midst at speed, with jubilant cries arising from within the stolen sedan as the bent oil-drum tumbled over the car's bonnet and embedded itself in the windscreen. The six drunken occupants spilled out of the vehicle before it had even ground to a halt, brandishing an assortment of cruel weapons as they then set about the stricken unfortunates.

"Hey!" a confident voice rang out as a lone male mounted the car roof, his long, grime-spattered coat flapping in his wake as he sprang through the air to close-line the first thug that turned his way.

At that, the rest of the gang ceased in their efforts to regard a rather scruffy-looking street-male of vaguely Asian origin standing over their fallen comrade; a smug sneer spread across his wolfish features as he casually drew on a cigarette before swigging from an undiluted bottle of bourbon.

"You're dead, man!" issued the burly gang leader, leveling a bloodied bat the youth's way as his peers closed in around him from all sides. "Kick his ass!"

The defiant young male flicked his cigarette directly into the eye of the first onrushing attacker to deter him and back-kicked another on his blindside, catching him clean in the throat to send him to ground. He then rolled with several well-aimed blows that come his way, deftly slipping among their arcs as he took another gulp from his bottle, before delivering three swift kicks that sent their recipients reeling from him in agony.

The leader, having first stood off to take stock of his opponent, attempted a flying tackle on the daring youth, crying out in frustration as the younger man leap-frogged over his back and sent him hurtling headfirst into the hull of the stationary vehicle with a derisive kick on the butt.

"Come on! That all you got!?" the youth crowed, looking on in disappointment as the thugs began backing away harboring the injuries already sustained. "I ain't even got started yet, boys."

"Try this on for size," muttered the dazed gang leader, arising from the ground with a small calibre handgun aimed his way.

The youth spun on him, hurling the bottle with all his might to shatter on the leader's skull, whereupon his wayward aim was directed at his fellow gang members, who cringed from the loud gunshot as their leader was felled. Even as the man crumpled to the ground, wiping blood from his eyes, the youth was upon him, hoisting him to his feet to issue three punches in rapid succession square across the man's jaw, only refraining from doing so when his unconscious form lay sprawled across the bonnet of the car.

"Any you ladies need a light?" he asked, a cigarette hanging from his lip as he flicked open his lighter to stand with it sparked over the inert alcohol-soaked body. "We bums gotta keep warm, you know?"

"Do it, kid," a bitter voice issued from the shadows, as several shambling figures emerged from the dilapidation all around him, their bloodshot eyes focused intently on the scene as the remaining thugs fled their wrath, abandoning their comrade to his fate.

"They'd do it to us," insisted another down-and-out.

Conflicting emotions weighed heavily on the surprisingly unmarred countenance of the young warrior as he contemplated carrying out the barbaric act, realizing how easy it would be for him to do so, and how much the scumbag deserved it. He stared into the heart of the tiny flame even as he stared into the deepest recesses of his soul to find the courage necessary to carry out the deed, soon rationalizing that the consequences, should the surviving gang members report him, would far outweigh the benefits and bring a lot of unwanted attention his way. There were secrets he would rather were kept hidden from the authorities, and the last thing he needed right now was the police looking for him.

"No," he replied, hanging up his lighter as he slung the gang leader over his shoulder. "We're better than that."

Cries of protest and indignation followed him as he promptly fled the area with his burden, his stride and pace somehow unaffected by the copious amounts of alcohol drunk earlier that night. He deposited the thug's body at the feet of his fellow gang members minutes later, who started in alarm as they cowered in the shadows nursing their wounds, fretting over the abandonment of their leader.

"The next time any of you pull this shit, I'll leave you back there for 'em after," he asserted, taking a long draw from a cigarette as he looked each of them in the eye. "Now, empty your pockets and give me any valuables you're carrying. You guys just worked me up an appetite."

# cloud

Catherine Baird

When I go to the cloud shop I know what I am looking for. I have a picture in my mind of my ideal cloud, but sometimes the ones I like are not available and I have to make do. I want to buy more and experiment with different ones and I have taken a course in how to make your own clouds.

A lot of tears are involved and you need an airtight room where you control the temperature so that your tears will become a small visible cloud above your head: a halo if you will, that represents all that is in your heart.

If your tears have been shed in sorrow, then they will produce a fluffy white cotton-wool cloud and if in anger and frustration the cloud will most likely be dark, tight, and brooding. If you have real sorrow but happen to be wearing mascara, then your perfect candyfloss will be streaked like Italian marble.

You can wear your cloud when you go out but it may not last very long and you should have some means of drying your hair. Or like old ladies used to, you could wear a rainmate. I saw someone last week with a brown cloud and although it was thick and dull, it suited her because she looked bored.

You can order up a light fluffy cloud to wear at funerals to show that you have real sorrow and that you are a nice person with no nasty side to you, but if you want to project a tough image you can get the angry ones; they are like a mini storm about to happen. Scientists are working on tiny dashes of lightning and rumbles of thunder but these will be uber expensive.

I am thinking of applying for a job as a cloud maker, I know a place where people order different coloured ones: pink or orange, but they have to spray the colour while the tearworker is crying and it can make you cough. The best tearmakers are women who have had a lot of sorrow in their lives and some women have been headhunted from countries where human suffering is at a premium. I am thinking of breaking up with my boyfriend to see if I get sadder. I need the extra money.

# Am Jist Fine

J. B. Quinn

Naw hen, a cannae stop tae blether the noo
A huv a doctor's appointment fur hauf-nine
An ma leg gets stiff if a staun too long
But apart fae that hen, am fine, am jist fine

Aye hen, it's ma hip, it's been gein' me gip
Am worried a won't make it up that incline
Auld age disnae arrive unaccompanied, ye know
But apart fae that hen, am fine, am jist fine

Weil, ma back's been botherin' me a bit
Nae a' ways, ye un'erstaun, but fae time tae time
A think it must be yon arthritis settin' in
But apart fae that hen, am fine, am jist fine

Mind, a think a need tae see an optician
A cannae read a newspaper an' that's a bad sign
Och, ma eyesight's been getting worse fur a while
But apart fae that hen, am fine, am jist fine

An' a'll huv tae get ma ears syringed
A canne hear a word wie these lugs a mine

A've goat tae turn the telly up full blast
But apart fae that hen, am fine, am jist fine

A wisnae o'er the door fur a week wie that flu
Aw naw... a'll huv tae go! Is that the time?
A'll be late an' huv tae wait in the queue
But apart fae that hen, am fine, am jist fine

Oan ma wie back, a'll drap in fur a chat
Get a couple a glasses oot an a'll get some rid wine
It's wan a ma five-a-day, an it's guid fur yer heart
It's thanks tae that hen, that am fine, am jist fine

# Memories Are Best Made Up

James A. Stewart

Night falls like a stone. The day-long dusk, fuelled by irradiated dust clouds, turns black. There is no halogen glow to light the streets and the weak illumination of the moon is imperceptible through the cloudy gloom. A pair of figures sit by the warm embers of a fire; she pokes the wood to coax the flames back into life. A howl in the distance echoes around the tunnel where they are sitting and sends shivers down their spines.

"How long has it been?" he asks.

"Fifteen years, maybe more. It's hard to say with no seasons." She sighs inwardly at the conversation repeating itself, once more.

"What happened?" Again it is he who asks the question. Despite the short sentence, it is still interspersed with coughs.

The howl roars up again, although still some distance away, it is closing in. She is poking the embers in an absent minded fashion with a stick in her left hand, using her right she pulls an imaginary tick from her left thigh, as if she has found a distraction. "War happened. It started in the East and spread from there."

"Why?"

"All those countries whom we had thought it right to place sanctions against joined forces against us. They attacked our nuclear facilities in a co-ordinated move. It was handfuls of small groups but maximum damage was inflicted."

He is lying in a sleeping bag, one she found in a derelict building earlier in the day. His cough incessant, she knew it had to be the radiation which was making him sick, she was certain of it. She felt fine; then again, she was about twenty years younger than him. For the last two years, since his accident, every night and every day has been a painful recitation of the same questions and answers. In the pre-War days he would have had access to medication and counselling, he would have been a patient somewhere; but today he is a millstone – a fact she does not want to admit.

He ended up like this as a result of a bang to the head he received when trying to outrun the Bugganes in a previous hunt. They had been forced to jump into a gorge, a sure way to shake off the chasing pack as they hated running water. The descent was less than ten feet, but the water was running fast enough to drag them about a mile downstream. It must have been during the time in the water that he took the fate-changing knock. She explains all of this to him after another set of oft asked questions. He just nods, not truly understanding the issue. He is completely unaware of the catastrophe which has befallen the planet; she assumes planet but for all she knows it may just be Britain.

"The last thing I can recall was going out for a drink for your birthday. Do you remember that?"

She throws more wood on the fire, the wood is dry and lifeless but sparks come instantly from the glowing fire.

She looks at him with affection, leaning over to pat his head. "I do. It was good. We had fun, and you were in great form. Can you remember singing the Frank Sinatra song?"

"Do I ever! *Bad Bad Leroy Brown.* I was good at mimicking old Frankie." He laughs as his eyes drift, picking over the bones of other memories.

"The next day all of this started." She says this as she points to the dark night and dust filled sky. The conversation is going down its usual path. But tonight she encourages it as a lump builds in her throat.

"And the government. What happened there?"

"They have given up, I expect. It became a case of self-preservation and for all I know Brown and Darling are in a bunker somewhere trying to re-establish authority, only in our time on the move I have seen nothing of the society we once knew. All that is left is chaos and disorder." She shudders as she finishes the last sentence, recalling some of the things she has done, some of the commodities she has had to trade for food, drink and shelter. "Nothing is sacred anymore. Nothing." she mumbles to herself.

Thunder claps in the distance as she stokes the fire still more. He shivers despite being in the warmth of the sleeping bag. He pulls the bag up to his neck before coughing his way through yet another question, "Who rules this place now, then?"

Shaking her head, she replies, "No one person or party. There is no central government, there is no single authority."

"So, is the whole world free?" He interrupts.

"No. There are some bad people, and things out there, that's all you need to know..."

Another howl, longer, stronger and closer shrills into the night air. "What is that?" he asks.

"That is a Buggane. They are mutated humans, cannibalistic and ferocious. It's OK, though, as long as I keep the flames burning they'll stay away." This time she throws some dried grass onto the fire to encourage the flames to lick the wood. She is lying.

He makes to sit up and ask a question but is forced back by a coughing fit. It lasts for nearly a minute, even with just the glow of the fire she can see the colour drain from his face. He spits up blood and closes his eyes for a few seconds, collecting himself, he looks her in the eye.

"This isn't the first time I have coughed up blood, is it?"

"No. It started a few weeks ago, it must be a sickness from the radiation. I have seen it before."

The fire is glowing well. The pair of them stare into it, transfixed by the warmth of the dancing flames. Howls pierce the night at regular intervals, some seem closer. Rain starts to fall lightly, and she is glad of the cover that the tunnel entrance provides.

He breaks the silence, "Are we just nuclear fall-out refugees, then?"

"Something like that. There are some survivors who chose to live a nomadic life, others set up camp under the jurisdiction of one of the area Lords. Others, like us, are scattered around the countryside."

Another coughing fit visits him, he spits up more blood. "So, what next for us?"

"Lord Macadon has sent hunters for those scattered, including us. He controls the Bugganes, they are his army. He allows them to hunt his land for refugees, it is a case of finder's keepers." She pauses as another howl pierces the air, it sounds like it has come from the other side of the burn which runs in front of their resting place. He attempts to rise again, concern shows in his face.

Raising her hand in a nonchalant manner, "Don't worry, they won't cross water unless on a bridge." She turns away to hide the fear in her face from him.

"It sounds like they are everywhere." He is trying to suppress the coughing in case it gives away their position. It only makes the eventual cackle louder and longer.

"They are. How are you feeling now?"

"I am fine, dear. The cough is not great but my head throbs. How did we get here?"

She explains, for the third time in a couple of hours how they got into the tunnel; about how they had to sneak past a handful of Bugganes; about how she knew this place to be strategically well placed. She tells him of Lord Macadon, The War and the loss of government. He nods, understanding but not remembering. And this is how it happens. In a flash, the conversation they are having ends abruptly and he is back to pre-war.

"I remember your party. It was a great night. I sang *Mack the Knife.* I'm good at that one," he says. His reminisces are ended by a screeching howl. It is nearby, less than one hundred yards, perhaps.

"What was that?" He tries to sit up but a coughing fit stops him, she gives him a comforting hug. She knows the Bugganes hunting them are getting nearer. Instinct and years of living wild tells her all she needs to know.

"It's a Buggane. One of those things I was telling you about earlier."

He looks distant, pale and tired. "Oh, I can't recall. Is it scary?"

She explains what the Bugganes are. She explains how they are mentally retarded and physically deformed humans under the control of Lord Macadon. She talks him through how the Lord came to power, goes into detail about how ruthless he is and how he rewards the Bugganes' loyalty by allowing them to kill strangers on his land. They, the Bugganes, skin and eat those caught. Every morsel is used: the skin for hides; the hair, teeth and ears for decoration. The bones are used as tools. She tells him of the Buggane who chased them into the gorge. How they got revenge for the injuries he suffered. He seems proud of memories he can't bring forth. She is lying but she wants to calm him, she wants him to be happy. The truth is they hid in a burrow for two days as the Buggane searched for them. At one point they could feel its footsteps above ground as they cowered underground. Sometimes the best memories are the made up ones.

He asks again, "How long has it been?"

She sighs, and continues to stoke the fire. She is mixing some water with a concoction of herbs she has collected. "Fifteen years, maybe more. It is hard to say with no seasons."

He coughs, it lasts a full minute. During this fit, howls screech from below and behind. He spits up more blood. She gets to her feet, finally taking her attention away from the fire. The howls frighten her now. Fork lightening brightens up the dark sky, making it look eerily red. She counts, one-two-three-four-five, before the thunder claps. The rain is getting heavier now, big droplets thud all around, they rat-a-tat on the roof of the tunnel and quickly turn the dirt at the foot of the entrance into mud.

"Are you scared?" he asks.

"Of course I am. I don't know what of, though. I don't know what the point is anymore."

"What scares you most? The Bugganes, howls and all, or looking after me, which I assume you do?"

"Don't..." Tears well up in her eyes. She looks at him; a life spent with each other flashes through her mind. She recalls how they pledged to stick together. He saved her life more times than she has digits to count up. He sacrificed himself for her; taking punishment, giving up food. He beat gangs who had attempted to rape her. To him, she is everything.

For her part, she loves him. She owes him everything.

He coughs again. The howls resonate around them. Even in the tunnel. She knows that there are multiple Bugganes on their tail. She guesses three, possibly four. She knows the hunters have made their position. She chides herself inwardly for not putting the fire down earlier, on a night like this it would be like a beacon. The noise from his regurgitations has most likely been heard, too. It is only a matter of time.

She finishes mixing the herb tea she has been making on the fire. She offers the cup to her companion. "Here, drink this. You'll feel better."

"Thank you." He drinks from the cup. His eyes look heavy and his palour weak. He sips from the cup as she gathers her belongings. He seems to understand what is happening. "Remember when I sang *That's Life* at your birthday party?"

She smiles at the innocence of the question. He is trying to make her happy. They couldn't get him off the karaoke that night, it was embarrassing at the time, but was in fact her last happy memory. And probably his also.

She looks into his eyes, "I do. It was wonderful and you were great at mimicking Frankie."

He puts his hand on her arm. "Goodbye, Jenny. I love you."

Sounds of footsteps and shrieks come from behind them in the tunnel. They are closing in fast. He smiles and closes his eyes, falling back and into the sleep she intended. His last sleep. She fights back the tears as she cradles him into position and kisses him on the forehead. A tear escapes and drops from her cheek onto his. The clamour behind her gets closer, perhaps less than fifty yards away. For the first time in her life she is alone.

"I love you, too, Dad." She says as she jumps off of the ridge and into the dark burn below, leaving his prone body to the carnivores.

# Early

Catherine Baird

Mary puts her Christmas decorations up
in November.
Harlequin flashes pulse through fake leaded windows.
Her children are 10, 8, and 6
and her husband is thirty-four years older than her.
The children never mention his grey hair or his teeth
in the glass by their toothbrushes:
WWF, Barbie and the other one.
The children have not seen him struggle
with his buttons, his tie,
nor Mary's face as he leaves for the office in the morning.
He's had two warnings.
They can't absorb his losses any more,
he has no insight into his condition.
the form says.
Mary knows. She has an understanding.
Gathering knowledge before she would really need it.
Dispensing tranquillisers to failed, grey souls
on wards in long-shut hospitals.
Mary puts the tree together, slotting
the metal ends of the branches into the upright central post,
spreading out the plastic pine needles,

each bauble in its place.
At hometime, the tree lit up
Mary watches for the sparkle in their eyes.
The children cavort around the lounge squealing
and turn off the big light.
The old man sits by the living-flame fire.
He will wonder where he is, in time,
and who these noisy little wretches are.
'Tea?' Mary says and leads him into the kitchen.
Mary keeps her hair the same so that he will know her

# Ma Maw

William N. Dyer

Ma maw died a few days before
Princess Diana.
Who remembers ma maw?

Ma maw had a hard life,
she was widowed twice before she was thirty three.
Who cares about ma maw?

Ma maw gave birth to five children,
she lost two before they were one.
Who gave solace to ma maw?

Ma maw brought me, my brother and sister
up to be honest, decent people.
Who laid flowers for ma maw?

Ma maw lived off *Provi* cheques
all her widowed days.
What state honours did she get?

Ma maw could have been famous.
She sang with a band in her youth,
voice of the devil in an angel's body.

Who gives a damn for ma maw's missed opportunity?

Ma maw loved her children,
I think we loved her too.
She did the best she could for us.
Who was there to mourn her passing?

Ma maw was a queen to me,
the only royalty that mattered.
No fake anything with ma maw.
Who was there at her end?

Ma maw would have had something to say
about Diana, Charles too.
I'm not sure how politically correct she'd have been.
Who would have cared what ma maw said?

Ma maw had too much experience
to have any affectations, to not tell the truth;
she was often wrong but it always felt right.
Who valued what she was?

Ma maw got the Alzheimer's,
I can't remember when it happened
but it crept up on her.
Who was there to watch her fade away?

Ma maw deserved better,
and so did your maw as well.
To be ignored because you're old and common place.
Who cares where you were when Diana died?

I;
I was with ma maw.

# Gaza

Catherine Baird

The Mediterranean sun is always a draw,
beating down and glinting off of the water.
You could pack up your raffia bag with lotion and towels
and head to the beach.
You could read your book,
you could lounge beside your lover and smile
from behind designer sunglasses.
You could breath deeply as your worries dissipate
in the heat of the day.
*Gaza is denied the means to clean its own sewage.*
You could take a trip in a glass-bottomed boat,
see the sea urchins,
the octopus corralled and stuck to the glass
by a diver.
You could take a photograph of its peachy, fleshy suckers.
*Millions of litres of raw sewage is dumped*
*into the sea surrounding Gaza every day.*
You could have an afternoon nap,
lounge with a glass of wine,
the grapes harvested from hot and windy fields
in Provence or La Rioja
before you dress for dinner.

A pavement café or
a tapas bar
eating the daily catch.
*Destruction of boats and related materials*
*has resulted in direct and indirect losses*
*of over two million dollars*
*to Gaza's fishing industry.*
Watching tourists wheel prams or stroll arm-in-arm
along the seafront
while the sun sets on the med.

# Burka

Danny O'Connor

I took Mohamet out in his pushchair. It was raining but mother-in-law likes to have us out of her house every day to give the baby fresh air. I was turning the corner and almost bumped into this man. He was wearing glasses and the wind was blowing the rain right at him. He didn't see me until the last second. When he got over his fright he threw me one of those looks I'm always catching from Westerners. It starts off as surprise and then turns into a too-long stare before they snap their heads round as though I'm not there.

Don't they realise I'm still a person inside this burka? I'm still flesh and blood and have all my feelings in the same places as their wives and daughters. Why do they show such disrespect to a religious woman? Mohamet wrote the Koran and the Imam teaches from the holy book that a girl who becomes, in body, a woman has to be more than modest when outside the protection of her family. She should not put herself in a position where she can inflame a man's passion. I know this teaching and I choose to wear a burka. I know that my hair and my face can send men wild with desire. I cover up so I do not arouse their passion.

Why can't the men of the west respect me like their Muslim brothers do? Don't they know that I live a religious life? Why do a frown and a sneer disfigure their features when I am in their sight? I am not of their culture and have no desire to flaunt my body wantonly like a wish-to-be page three girl and show my breasts and my navel to all who walk the street. For I know that I will be punished by Allah if I do this. These western women have not yet heard the word of the true God but when they do, and that day will surely come, they too will wish to cover themselves from the sight of strangers or they too will surely feel the lash of Allah's wrath.

# Coatbridge

Catherine Baird

Taking my hand, my grandmother steps onto the road in between two buses. She drags me over to the other side of the street. I know I am in Coatbridge because I have been here before. I don't really like my grandmother; she always pulls at my collar and complains about how dirty my neck is. She keeps photographs of me and my brothers but they are in the bedroom out of the way and I am conscious of myself when she looks at them. She always says how untidy my hair is in the pictures, she says it is like rats' tails. In the livingroom she has lots of photos of my cousin. His hair is always neat. My grandmother tugs me along the main street, into the butchers. There is a smell in here that I am not sure if I like or not. It is dry and wet at the same time and I watch the butcher as he picks up the pound and a half of steak mince and puts it onto white paper that is the same as the toilet paper in my grandmother's bathroom. All of the women in the queue have message bags. I know what women put in their message bags as I often play with my grandmother's when I visit her. She has hankies at the bottom in a plastic wrapper and I like to pretend that they are hospital quilts for my smallest dolls. She has a rainmate in her bag and I have watched her put it on over her hat when she thinks it might rain. I don't like wearing two hats but I suppose I will when I am a lady. My grandmother's bag is where she keeps her purse. It is a yellow brown colour and has a clasp that is dark metal. She always has lots of money. I am pulled into bootsthechemist where she waits on a seat beside the medicine counter. I sit on the chair next to her and she tells me to get up because the chairs are for adults. She says I can sit on her knee but I don't want to. She has fat knees and she is warm, but if I sit on her knee sometimes she gets up in a hurry and pushes me off without warning. My other grandmother is skinny and if I sit on her knee I feel that I might squash her. But she never pushes me off and sometimes lets me fall asleep. She never complains about my neck and has my photograph on the sideboard behind the couch. After bootsthechemist we go back towards the bus stop and I think we are going home, but she takes me into the Co-operative store and says we are going for a cup of tea. I like the Co-operative. It is busy and hot and there are great big lights that hang down from the ceiling, swaying on long wires. They are like the lights in the church and some have missing bulbs. She makes me sit at a table with all of the shopping and my grandfather's prescription. It is Valium. I read the bottle before; I am quite a good reader. But I don't think she should give it to him because I think it is this medicine that makes him all shaky. When my grandmother comes back to the table she tells me to sit up straight and gives me a glass of milk and a hot cross bun. It is nearly Easter and hot cross buns are in all of the bakers' windows. It is not my favourite, but my grandmother says it has something to do with god and puts butter on it for me. I see Kitty coming up the stairs into the Co-operative café. She is my grandmother's neighbour and I like her. She has goosegogs in her garden and I am allowed to pick them with her grandchildren when I am visiting. She never looks at my neck for dirt and I have never sat on her knee. Kitty gets a hot cross bun too and joins us with her small silver pot of tea. She says it is a bad pourer. They talk about my mother and I have time to daydream without my grandmother telling me to get a move on, or how I should try to be ladylike when I eat.

# Notes on the Contributors

***Catherine Baird*** writes poetry, drama and prose. She lives in North Lanarkshire with her husband and son and is currently studying Journalism and Creative Writing at the University of Strathclyde. Her work has most recently appeared in the inaugural edition of Glasgow literary magazine, *Gutter*.

***Alexander J. Cunningham*** has more ideas than he knows what to do with. Within the pages of this collection are just three from a larger work entitled *Cityscape*, a linked mosaic of scenes, characters, events and that take place within the sandbox of a fictional and ever growing city. Alexander has written many other works, from poetry collections, scripts and screenplays to several novels, though often finds new ideas rising up, before he can complete the work of the previous new idea.

***William N. Dyer*** is a teacher of computing, a student of life, and a writer who is striving to be as good as he can be. He sees failures as necessary steps on the journey to success. Taking that journey started a few years ago and it's not too late, it's never too late.

***Samuel McCann*** is Cumbernauld native who has lived in Australia and Malaysia, but who always ends up back in the new town somehow. He has been a member of the Frontier Writers group for six years and enjoys writing in the supernatural, fantasy and super-powered genres, and this is reflected in his two pieces included in this collection.

Renegade is a prologue introducing a new character for use in the sequel to his novel, *Legacy of the Dragon*, and Triple Threat Treat was a bit of fun in the pulp horror genre.

***Eddie McGonnell*** retired from full-time employment three years ago and has found the Frontier Writers Group to be a wee Shangri-La of companionship and fertile writing ideas. The writing and what is discussed is always interesting and he feels he has benefited from the rapport and understanding of his fellow scribes. He is also a keen movie buff and feels that his awareness of film has been greatly enhanced by the flood of literary ideas emanating from the group. He is married with three sons and two young grandsons. Eddie hopes that the group will continue to flourish for many years to come and thanks his colleagues for putting up with his meagre literary contribution.

***Erin McHugh*** has always enjoyed writing and mainly writes lyrics because she finds it a fun and easy way to express herself. The first of her poems in this collection is a lighthearted piece about a childhood memory, whilst the second expresses her views on the degradation of our civil liberties. She writes about whatever comes to mind and sees it as a way to reflect and learn about herself. For Erin, writing is a cheap alternative to therapy. She says you can feel the whole spectrum of human emotion, and put pen to paper in a bid to enjoy and handle what life throws at you.

***Craig Murray*** writes poetry and song lyrics. His work is inspired by emotions felt in real situations. He tries to write light-hearted, happy poetry, but invariably, like looking for love and settling for lust, his work often ends up in dark and brooding places.

***Danny O'Connor*** is now a grey goatee as Maureen, the love of his life, never has been too keen on a full beard. After a hiatus of about 3 years he has come back to writing poetry since Feb. this year. He is now totally addicted to performance poetry and *getting laughter* from his works is *like a drug*. He will have to go cold-turkey one day but for now he's enjoying the journey one day at a time. All the live segments of his upcoming poetry CD are now *in the can,* but he is dragging his feet with selecting the poems for the studio. He also thinks he can write in a literary fashion. He sold a science fiction short story and that now makes him a semi-professional writer. He fell into flash fiction and now writes autobiography in 50 word segments.

***J. B. Quinn*** considers herself a lazy writer and says that poetry for her is a relatively easy process. It is her preferred literary medium for commenting on important issues. She uses the form of the poem to explore unorthodox ideas and feels this affords her the speed of thought she needs.

***Hugh Reynolds*** is what one can only describe as haphazard or a now-and-again type of writer. He writes short stories he thinks sometimes are brilliant, but after much deliberation and rewrites they usually end up deleted. Never fear, everyone loves a trier! With a lot of encouragement from the other group members in Frontier

Writers group in Cumbernauld he is in with a shout of creating something *interesting!* His most recent publishing success came in the 2008 edition of the respected anthology, *New Writing Dundee.*

***James A. Stewart*** is a career Croy boy. He sees himself as a lifelong student and regards joining Frontier Writers in 2008 as one of the smartest moves he has made. He lives with his bonnie wife and bairn in, you guessed it, Croy. As well as this publication, during 2009 his work has appeared in print in places such as *Static Movement, Chimeraworld 6, First Edition, Sex and Murder* and he has pieces due to appear in *Whortleberry Press Christmas in Space, Encountered Magazine* and *Delivered Magazine.*

***Claire Szemis*** is a journalism graduate from Glasgow Caledonian University. She has been writing short stories for most of her life and has won awards in a number of competitions. In 2002 she was 1st place in the North Lanarkshire Writer of the Year Intermediate section (12-18 years) and the following year she was runner-up in the adult's group. Recently she has been writing a series of currently unpublished novels, and her pieces in this collection are excerpts from that series.

***Jacqueline Woods*** left high school with passes in various subjects thereafter, she studied English at the University of Strathclyde. Here she became very interested in the dramatic arts, which she studied as part of her university course. At this time she also began to participate in productions and workshops with Strathclyde Theatre

Group, and is still involved in theatrical pursuits. An avid reader, she enjoys fiction and biographies, and also poetry. She is currently studying Media and Art part-time at college and works as an Administrative Officer.

# Acknowledgments

- Gordon Hughes for unstinting and indefatigable support of the group
- Muirfield Centre for giving us the physical space in which to share our ideas and work
- All of our friends and loved ones who have put up with us during the production of this collection